MW00331001

SPECTERS

Jeff Gelb

BART

NEW YORK

Copyright © 1988 by Jeff Gelb

Reprinted by arrangement with the author.

ISBN: 1-55785-015-1

First Bart Books edition: 1988

Bart Books
155 E. 34th Street
New York, New York 10016

Manufactured in the United States of America

The first one's for
Mike Garrett. I couldn't
have done it without you.
Now it's your turn!

"The devil hath power
   to assume a pleasing shape."

WILLIAM SHAKESPEARE,
Hamlet, act 2, scene 2, p. 628

Prologue

August 1968, Cape Cod

Joseph Simmons was thirty feet into the surf before he slackened his pace to a slow crawl. He took big gulps of salty air and then dove under the sky-blue surface. He opened his eyes but could see nothing beneath his toes— this far out, the Atlantic's bottom was at least fifty feet below him.

Simmons rolled onto his back and let the salty ocean water carry his weight while he gazed at the puffy cloud formations overhead. Even for the Cape, it was a gorgeous summer day, and an invigorating swim was just what he needed to reflect on past victories and future triumphs.

A smile crossed his handsome features. Things were going beautifully for him. His move from journalist to politician a dozen years ago, when he was thirty, had been a remarkably smooth transition. His obvious intelligence, charm, and aggressive attitude had contributed to what other reporters had called his "meteoric rise." First mayor of Boston, then governor of Massachusetts, and now he'd been named the Democratic candidate for the 1968 Presidential election.

Simmons flipped onto his stomach and began an even-paced breast stroke farther away from shore and the beach house where Sondra was making lunch. As he swam, he thought of his wife, a pert blonde he'd met on the campaign trail years ago. He was proud of Sondra. She was both attractive and smart, and he knew that she had gained him many votes from both sexes.

1

The smile on his full lips compressed as he thought of the upcoming elections. His liberal attitudes were nearly legendary by now, and while those beliefs had helped Simmons attain his current status, he was wondering now whether the mood of the country was swinging back to a more traditional bent.

It was 1968 and the war in Viet Nam was escalating. Teenage boys were fighting and dying without really understanding what the war was all about. At his most recent speeches, Simmons had noted some disagreement over his strongly held antiwar sentiments. He knew the veterans were against him because he wanted to bring the American troops home and let the war resolve itself without further U.S. intervention. He'd even received some death threats, but took these no more seriously than any of the crank letters that all politicians received daily. Sondra, however, had become noticeably upset over the anonymously-written threats. So, Simmons had decided to take a break from the campaigning and visit their favorite retreat here at the Cape. His campaign manager had bitched and his security adviser had panicked: It was too close to the elections, there was no time to adequately prepare for his safety, etcetera etcetera.

Simmons grimaced and increased his stroke. He felt his heart beat as he turned toward the shoreline. He'd almost let his good-intentioned staff talk him out of this trip, but in the end, the fear in his wife's eyes had decided for him.

He was thinking of Sondra's pretty face when something struck his foot. He gasped and pulled away, then dove under the surface to see what had bitten him. His eyes were tearing too much to see in the salty water. God damn, it hurt! His foot already felt like it had ballooned to twice its normal size. Each pulse sent a bolt of pain stabbing up his leg. He surfaced for air.

He was having trouble controlling the stricken leg. It was totally unresponsive to his commands, instead doing some kind of crazy dance.

The pain suddenly seemed to be coming from all over his body. Simmons found himself sweating profusely, his heart beating a wild, erratic rhythm. He was having trouble breathing. Calm down, dammit!

He realized he was in danger of drowning and blinked in stunned disbelief. It was impossible . . . he had come so far . . . he was so close . . . there was so much left to be done . . .

He tasted the salty water and was astonished to find himself below the water's surface. He was confused. Which way was up? Follow your goddamned air bubbles! he berated himself. You can do that much, can't you?

Was he sinking? It was so damned dark down here. But . . . so peaceful. He started to laugh, tasted the sickeningly salty water. Simmons knew he was losing consciousness, but the fight was out of him.

His eyes bulged and the muscles in his throat relaxed. A small fish swam into his mouth, changed its mind, and swam out again. Simmons floated downward, arms waving slowly above him in a silent farewell to life.

On the shore, behind a sand dune, sunlight glinted off dual circles of glass. Wind swallowed the sounds of laughter.

Part One

THE GIFT

Chapter One

1988

Carlo Filippo stood up, cleared his throat, and struck a sterling silver knife repeatedly against a crystal water goblet. His dinner guests quickly turned their attention to him.

"I'm not very good at speeches," he stammered. "You all know why you're here and what we're celebrating." He looked down at his wife, seated beside him. "If it weren't for all of you, Christina and I wouldn't be here right now. Not together, anyway."

Christina Filippo returned her husband's loving smile. "What Carlo's trying to say is that you've all been the best of friends to us and we're so grateful . . ." Tears came to the corners of her eyes. She dabbed at them with her cloth napkin and continued.

"It's no secret to any of you that Carlo and I were on the verge of divorce last year. You know how hot-tempered we Italians can be." There was a chorus of laughs from the guests.

Carlo raised a glass of deep red wine toward a man who had the rugged good looks of a performer in a cigarette advertisement. "Robert, you saw our relationship falling apart day by day. I was allowing work to consume my life. I had become a horrible husband to Christina and a failure as a father to Vic." He nodded in the direction of their teenage son's bedroom, where the guests could hear muffled rock music.

"Robert," Carlo continued, "you and Cheryl were the first to sit us down and talk about what you saw happening between us. You encouraged us to seek professional help." Under the table, Cheryl Richardson, a lookalike for Jane Fonda in her *Klute* days, gave her husband's knee a playful squeeze. Robert diverted his gaze from Christina Filippo, who was winking at him conspiratorially.

Carlo turned to face his next two guests. "Louis, your contacts at the university enabled you to recommend our 'personal savior,' Dr. Sanders here. For that, I am forever in your debt." Louis Silver, a tall, thin-faced serious type with thick glasses, clinked wineglasses with Carlo and the two took small sips. Louis's wife Virginia gave her husband a peck on the cheek.

"You know how these college psych profs are," she said. "They love to give advice."

Their host refilled his glass and tilted it in the direction of the big, bearded man at the other end of the table who resembled Sebastian Cabot. "Michael, as our psychologist and counselor, you did what no other man had ever done to me before: you told me that I was full of shit!"

Dr. Sanders's broad face loosened into a grin. "Just doing my job."

"You're too modest, doctor. Wouldn't you agree, Mrs. Sanders?" The plain-faced woman to Sanders's left nodded unenthusiastically as Filippo continued. "To all of you, this dinner party is dedicated. And I would now like to return all of your favors. Christina and I have decided to celebrate our newfound love symbolically by renewing our vows while on a cruise to the Bahamas."

Robert Richardson slapped Carlo's back good-naturedly. "Great idea," he said.

Carlo smiled. "My wife and I would be most honored if you would all be our guests."

Carlo laughed as he watched his guests react to the invitation: six sets of eyebrows were raised, six mouths dropped in shock.

"That's hardly necessary, Carlo," said Dr. Sanders.

"We're all happy to see the two of you back on track. Surely that is reward enough."

Carlo brought his glass down hard on the marble table-top. "I'm not accustomed to being argued with." He blinked and softened his tone. "Listen to me, all of you. I'm a rich man, and you know it. If I don't spend my ill-gotten money on my friends, I'll only waste it on myself sooner of later. Please let me . . . let us do this." He put an arm around his wife, who nodded toward their guests.

The table fell silent. Finally Robert Richardson shrugged and said, "Well, certainly the Bahamas in February beats the pants off snowbound Rochester, New York. The hell with guilt trips. Let's show the Filippos how to have a really great time!"

"Bravo," yelled Carlo. He maneuvered the red wine bottle over each of his guest's glasses, then raised his own for another toast. "To my friends, old and new—the best friends in the world."

"And to you and your lovely wife—and a new beginning," answered Dr. Sanders.

Several bottles of rich Italian red wine later, the dinner guests had moved to the sunken living room. Louis challenged Robert to a video game on Carlo's big-screen TV. Dr. Sanders examined the room's huge library, thumbing through one of the hundreds of books on architecture that Carlo had read along the way to becoming one of the world's best-known industrial designers. Virginia and Cheryl sat together on a plush silk couch, discussing their favorite nighttime soap opera. Betty Sanders sat in a corner, crocheting a quilt square.

Carlo poured his wife another glass of wine despite her slurred protests.

"Carlo, I'll feel awful in the morning."

He grinned and downed the contents of his wineglass in a single gulp. "It's tonight I'm thinking about." He kissed her as one of his hands found her ample bosom.

Christina glanced at her guests, who were all involved

in various activities. "Let's do it right now," she whispered as she nibbled on his ear and ran her hand over the bulge in his pants.

Without a word, Carlo rose and took his wife's hand, leading her out of the living room and down the hall.

Shutting their bedroom door behind them, he turned to see his wife slipping out of her dress. Moments later, she was nude and lying on their satin-sheeted bed. She cupped her breasts and whispered, "Carlo, my love . . ."

"Wish someone would tell that *boy* to turn down his stereo," Betty Sanders complained to no one in particular.

Her husband laughed embarrassedly. "Betty's never been a fan of rock and roll," he complained.

"Or teenagers," she added out of the corner of her thin mouth.

Dr. Sanders grimaced at that, actually forming two tight fists with his hands. His wife's eyes bulged momentarily and she reverted her attention to her crocheting project.

"I love teenagers," Sanders went on, acutely aware that everyone in the room was watching him intently. "Betty and I are unable to have children of our own, you know." His wife almost gave him an evil eye, thought better of it, and continued her knitting. "That's why I decided to make child psychology my area of specialty," he continued, feeling the need to justify himself to his friends.

"And you've made quite a name for yourself," Louis Silver said, patting his friend's hunched shoulder.

"Not the same as having children of my own, though," Sanders mumbled almost to himself.

Cheryl Richardson chimed in, "I agree with Betty. I swear, rock and roll is all our kids listen to. It's enough to drive any sane person crazy. I think it's already gotten to our boy . . ."

"Cheryl!" her husband Robert reprimanded her. "There's nothing wrong with Johnny. Honestly, you sound like our *parents*! Don't you remember the crap they gave us for listening to 'Elvis the Pelvis' and Little Richard . . ."

"I thought those guys were creepy," Virginia said, coming to Cheryl's defense. "Now Pat boone . . . Gene Pitney . . . they were dreamboats!"

"That's my wife," Louis laughed. "Square as the day is long."

The conversation continued, breaking into diverse groups. No one noticed a form make its way silently down the hall, his destination a den at its opposite end.

His eyes fell on a large pile of logs. Next to them, an axe was propped against the wall. The blade gleamed in the firelight's reflection.

He dug into his pocket and brought out a pair of dishwashing gloves. He pulled them on, then picked up the axe, shifting its weight from one hand to another. It fell strong enough.

He strode silently back down the hall, axe held behind one leg. Sweat beaded his brow. He had to move quickly.

He cupped an ear against the bedroom door, hearing rhythmic squeaks and groans. Inside, the bed protested softly as Christina sat astride Carlo's bulging midriff, moving up and down in a slow, sensuous rhythm. Carlo's eyes were closed in ecstasy, while Christina stared into space. The two were grunting in unison.

"I'm almost there . . . don't come without me," Christina panted, her tongue slightly protruding from parted lips. Carlo groaned in response.

The form was in the bedroom by now, inching his way toward the bed from a far wall. His knuckles were white from their grip on the axe handle.

"Oh my God," Carlo panted through tightly shut eyes. "I can't wait anymore!"

The two gasped and surrendered to a thunderous mutual orgasm.

The intruder hoisted the axe high above his head and, with all his might, brought it down. The keen blade sliced through the flesh and bone of Carlo's neck like a knife through warm butter. The axe continued its downward arc and carved its way through a second neck. Two heads fell in opposite directions and the murderer quickly stepped back to avoid the blood, spurting out of exposed veins in a wild rush.

The killer realized he'd been holding his breath since he'd entered the room. His vision was blurring and he felt like he was going to faint. He took big gulps of air and let a wall support his weight until his vision cleared and his heart slowed down. He dropped the axe on the bloodied bedsheets and strode to the door. He peeked into the hallway. It was empty.

He ran to the bathroom, flushed the gloves down the toilet, and washed his hands. He toweled dry and wiped the sweat from his brow.

It was ten minutes later when someone remarked about the absence of the party's hosts. Robert Richardson quipped, "If I know those hot-blooded Italians, all that booze went straight to their libidos."

"Kind of rude of them, isn't it?" asked Cheryl.

"Don't fool yourself, honey. I think we're all ready to hit the sack . . . with or without sex. It is getting kind of late."

"Should we tell them we're going?" Virginia queried.

Her husband Louis shrugged. "We'll just lock the door on the way out." As the group made its way to the front entrance, Virginia placed a restraining hand on her husband's arm.

"Shouldn't we see if . . . everything's all right?"

Louis sighed. "My wife . . ." he laughed. "Okay, if it will make you feel better. But I'll lay odds they're either sleeping or doing something we should be doing right about now . . ." He walked down the hallway to the master bedroom, where he could see a sliver of light shining from under the closed door. He knocked softly.

"You guys up?" Louis noticed an odd smell in the hallway, like strong cheese that had been left out of the refrigerator. Maybe something was wrong with the house's central air-conditioning. He'd mention it to Carlo.

Louis opened the door a crack. The room was awash in

blood and excrement. When he saw the Filippos' headless bodies, his dinner flew into his throat.

He weaved and took a slow fall to the plush gray carpeting. The last thing he saw before blacking out was Christina's head, staring at him upside down on the rug.

Chapter Two

The night was sleepless for the Filippos' party guests and for their son Vic. When the endless police questions finally dwindled, cold dawn was already breaking over the snowy Rochester skyline.

Dr. Michael Sanders closed his office for the day, had a long discussion with his wife, and offered the police his services as legal guardian to Vic Filippo until things were straightened out.

Louis Silver threw himself into bed, shivering with a fever he knew was not from a flu bug, but from shock. Virginia ran a cold washcloth over her husband's creased forehead, dreading the morning's questions from her son Paul, still asleep in the next room.

At the Richardson residence, Cheryl kept her mind busy by preparing breakfast for Robert and her children. All three were reading the morning paper; Robert the sports section, fourteen-year-old Johnny the comics page, fifteen-year-old Annette the fashion page.

Grief and the night's terror finally took their toll, as Cheryl dropped the egg beater into the cat's food dish. The Persian looked at the woman in disgust and walked away from its ruined breakfast. Cheryl broke into a series of heaving sobs and ran out of the room.

Robert made her lie down on the couch while he fetched a Valium. After she was settled, with a mystified Annette by her side, Robert rejoined Johnny at the breakfast table.

The boy's curly-haired head was buried in the comics section in an attempt to ignore the bad vibes in the house. He was desperately scared that his homeroom teacher had called—Johnny'd been skipping classes a lot lately to hang around with his older buddy Vic.

Johnny was almost relieved when his father explained that his friend Vic's parents had been killed. Lately, news stories involving deaths had fascinated Johnny Richardson. He'd even started trading luridly violent comic books and paperbacks with Vic, against his parents' wishes.

"What happened to them, Dad?"

"Johnny, I'm . . . not allowed to say. The police are still investigating."

Johnny noticed has father's hand shaking as he lifted the coffee mug to his lips.

"Is Vic okay?" Johnny asked, almost as an afterthought.

"He's . . . had quite a shock, Johnny. I think it's going to take some special attention over a long period of time before Vic is his old self again. He . . . may live with a doctor for a while . . . someone who can help him through this." Robert set the mug down and stared at it silently. Finally, he shook himself out of his reverie.

"Aren't you going to be late for school? The bus should be coming any minute."

Johnny reluctantly quit the table and grabbed his coat and books. His father ran a hand through Johnny's hair, but the boy pulled away in annoyance.

Robert remained at the door, watching the retreating form of his son. Johnny was a younger version of his father: strong chin, dark eyes, thin lips, not an ounce of fat anywhere on his lithe frame. Robert was desperately proud of the boy and blindly in love with him. If anything were to ever happen to his only son . . .

Robert's hand shook as he closed the door. That Valium didn't sound like such a bad idea.

By the time Johnny arrived at Brighton Junior High School, the news of the Filippo deaths was the main topic of conversation in the halls. Before the end of the day,

Johnny had heard his teachers whispering the word "decapitation" more than once.

Johnny walked home that day, slowing down as he passed by Brighton High School. He stopped when he saw Arnie Brenner, a fat kid with a skin problem who hung around with Vic.

"Hear what happened to Vic's parents?"

Johnny nodded. "How's Vic?"

"Dunno. Gonna try and see him later tonight. Hear how they got offed?"

Johnny thought he knew, but wanted confirmation from another source. Arnie drew an index finger in an imaginary line across his neck, let his head flop to one side, and stuck his tongue out of one corner of his grinning mouth.

"Gross, huh?"

Johnny nodded as a shiver ran down his spine. He started to walk away and heard Arnie laughing behind him. As soon as Johnny had rounded the corner, he started running, and didn't stop till he reached home. Maybe death wasn't so funny after all.

That night, Johnny dreamed he was running through a sea of oatmeal, feverishly trying to escape a laughing hooded figure brandishing a bloodied axe.

"Leave me alone!" Johnny screamed. "Get out of my head!"

The figure caught Johnny's hair, tilted his head back so the boy's smooth white neck was showing, the bobbing Adam's apple providing a perfect target . . .

"I need you," whispered the form, and lowered the axe.

Johnny awoke to the sickening smell of wet bedsheets.

When the paper arrived the next morning, Johnny beat his father to the front porch to pick it up. He'd just located the Filippo story when his dad grabbed the paper out of his hands.

"Jesus," he whispered as he glanced over his father's shoulders to read the sensational front-page headline: "Double Decapitation Deaths!'' A black-and-white photo showed the empty, blood-soaked bed, with the murder weapon laying across the sheets.

Johnny's eyes bulged as he looked at the photo. He'd have to add that one to his collection! He stayed silent till his father finished reading the story and put down the paper.

''Who killed 'em, Dad?''

''No one knows, Johnny.''

''Do you think the killer was in the house during the party, Dad? You know, like maybe waiting in a closet or something?''

''Jesus, Johnny, I don't know. Anything's possible. Eat your breakfast.''

''I'm not hungry.''

''Then get ready for school.''

Johnny was silent for a beat, then asked, ''Is it okay if I go with you to the funeral? You know, to be with Vic. He's probably all messed up.''

Robert considered the request. He didn't really like the Filippo kid, whom he felt was spoiled rotten and a bad apple to begin with.

''I'll think about it.''

Johnny grinned. His first funeral! Now that was going to be way cool!

He'd already forgotten his nightmare.

Later that night, while his mother and father watched *The Cosby Show,* Johnny snuck into the kitchen and sifted through the garbage pail till he came up with the front section of the morning paper. He wiped off some egg stains from the paper and carefully cut out the entire article on the Filippo murders.

Johnny ran up to his room and, grabbing a flashlight, crawled under his bed, where he taped the article to the underside of his mattress. With the flashlight standing on end, he read the article and looked at the photo over and over again. Finally, having memorized the details of the incident, he let his vision wander to the other articles and photos he'd carefully clipped from other newspapers and magazines over the past six months. It was his own private rogue's gallery. His best-kept secret.

Chapter Three

Over eight months passed with no arrests in the Filippo case. Yet somehow life settled down for those affected by the tragedy. The Sanders were court-appointed as guardians to Vic Filippo, much to Mrs. Sanders's regret and her husband's delight. The Silvers and Richardsons agreed not to discuss the murders, while their sons seemed to have lost interest in them. There were other things to occupy young minds. It was, after all, the eve of Halloween.

Johnny Richardson propelled his BMX racer down the quickly darkening streets of his neighborhood. He cut sharply to the right as he spotted the rusted iron gates of Mt. Hope cemetery, a sprawling collection of tombstones, spires, and mausoleums. The gates were already locked, but Johnny had explored the cemetery enough times to have found a part of the surrounding wall that had crumbled and never been repaired.

He looked at his watch: 8:10. His parents wouldn't expect him till nine, when he said he'd be home from playing at Paul's house. Johnny smiled as he thought of his best friend. Johnny and Paul Silver had grown up together—his parents and Paul's had gone to high school together and had remained friends and neighbors ever since.

Johnny cut his bike light and rode by the ample illumination of the emerging full moon, expertly navigating the tiny roads within the cemetery. He was pedaling slowly, attention focused on the passing crypts. Finally, in a section of the cemetery where the grass had grown taller than some of the stone markers, he spotted a crypt with its door slightly ajar. Johnny dropped his bike in the overgrowth and made his way to the crypt.

He peered inside, smelling musty darkness, then took out the cigarette lighter he'd found on the street last week and stuck it through the narrow opening.

He brought out his hand with a yelp—spiderwebs! Then he felt the spider itself, a gigantic black thing with white stripes on an enormous body. It was crawling up his arm! Johnny screamed and shook his arm wildly, dropping both the spider and cigarette lighter.

"Shit!" He wasn't about to bend down and look for the lighter with that spider somewhere at his feet. He'd just have to hope the moonlight provided ample light inside the crypt.

Johnny pushed open the door and inched his way into the darkness beyond. He shut his eyes and counted slowly to ten, then opened them again. He could see much better now. He was standing between two stone caskets, and he was in luck: the lid of one was slightly cracked from age.

He giggled. He was going to make this Halloween something very special for his buddy Paul! He'd been planning this gag ever since he'd attended the Filippo funeral.

Johnny checked his luminous watch dial: 8:30. He'd better hurry. He examined the space between the cracks in the coffin lid. It was just barely wide enough to stick his hand through.

Johnny gulped, afraid to stick his hand down there. Maybe there were more spiders. Or worse. And what condition was the corpse itself in? Would he touch scraps of clothing and bones, or wrinkled, leathery flesh.

For a moment, Johnny wished he could just forget this crazy idea, run out of that creepy crypt and ride like the wind back home. Then he'd tear all the newspaper articles from under his bed, throw away the monster magazines and horror comics, and be normal again. Normal—like he was before he turned thirteen and started to feel some strange signs of oncoming puberty . . . including his sudden interest in death and dismemberment.

But the moment came and went, like a cool breeze weaving through a parched desert.

Johnny took a big gulp of air, held it, and stuck his hand into the coffin crack. It was cold down there.

He heard a squeal and brought his hand out so quickly that he scraped it against the edge of the crack. What the hell was that? Now he heard other noises from within the coffin: a furious scraping and bumping. Johnny's eyes bulged and he danced away from the coffin. Something hit the back of his leg and he went over backward, hitting the cold stone floor with a hard thud.

Suddenly, he saw tiny fingers cresting the top of the coffin lid. Johnny pushed himself farther back into a corner and squinted while his heart hammered out a frenetic rhythm. They weren't fingers—they were claws! And now an engorged stomach, and a long tail. It was a rat, then another, and a third, all jumping out of the coffin's cracked lid and over the side.

He heard them hit the floor with slaps of sound. One squealed and then there was total silence. The light of the moon did not reach the floor of the crypt.

Something brushed against Johnny's hand. He leaped to his feet and ran to the coffin, scrambling atop of it. He rapped against the lid. No sound came from within. He bent down and yelled into the coffin, "Hey, Willard, you down there?" He half expected to see a giant rat come bounding out of the coffin, but none did. And in a moonlit corner of the room, he saw a small form scurry through a hole in the foundation.

Johnny wiggled two fingers into the crack, then stuck his hand down till it touched something hard. He pulled at it but it wouldn't give. He pulled again, harder, and heard a sharp crack, like a twig breaking. He brought his hand out with its prize, and held it up to the moonlight. Perfect! And whoever was down there sure wasn't going to miss it.

The boy stuck a tentative toe down to the floor and swished it in either direction. No sounds of movement.

Johnny jumped down, scooted across the floor in great bounds, and scrambled out the door.

He was home on the dot of nine, ran up to his room, shut and locked his door, and crawled under his bed. He turned on the flashlight and examined his prize, a wide grin splitting his face. He shivered with excitement—he was going to have great fun tomorrow night

Halloween night.

Chapter Four

Paul screamed and screamed. His father threw the newspaper against the wall, jumped out of his armchair, and bounded upstairs.

He shook his son, awakening him. A sheen of sweat made Paul slippery to his father's touch.

"Hey, Sparky, no problem! Dessert give you nightmares or what?"

Paul blinked, glanced around the room, and then into his father's bespectacled eyes. He blushed. "Guess I fell asleep reading."

"That's some wicked dream you must've been having."

A cloud passed over Paul's eyes momentarily. "I dreamed I was drowning . . . only it wasn't me, really. It was like I was sitting in someone else's body, and he was drowning."

Louis frowned. "Anybody we know?"

Paul shook his head, the long, straight black hair whisking across his shoulders. His eyes regarded his father with the sparkle that had caused Louis to nickname Paul "Sparky."

"It's okay, Dad," he smiled. "Really."

Louis stood up and stretched. "Well then . . . you better get going if you don't want to be late."

Paul's eyes bugged as he noticed the time: 7:45. "Shit!" He blushed, his thin face darkening deeply. "Sorry, Dad." Paul leaped off his bed and grabbed a pile of rags from the floor by his closet. He began to disrobe and then to put on the torn pieces of clothing.

His father frowned. "What kind of outfit is that?"

"It's gonna be real neat, Dad. Johnny and I are both dressing up as zombies. You know, like in *Night of the Living Dead*. I'm gonna put on makeup and everything. Wait'll you see!"

Louis shook his head slowly. "Times change," he muttered as he exited the room. "Yell when you're ready and I'll drive you over to Johnny's."

"Thanks, Dad." Paul was already absorbed in applying makeup.

"Have fun," Louis yelled from the car. Paul pounded on the front door of Johnny's parents' split-level home. Louis stayed until the door was answered by Johnny, who looked as grotesque as Paul in his makeup. Louis clucked his tongue and drove away. He wondered whether Paul was being adversely influenced by Johnny; the boy seemed a bit obsessed with monsters. But then, it was Halloween.

As he drove, Louis pushed back the cobwebs in his memory to his own Halloween masquerades, when he would dress as a hobo or a clown and go from door to door. Sometimes he would be rewarded with handmade caramel apples, other times taffy or hard candies, which he disliked and traded with friends. He remembered what a treat it was when a neighbor would give him a full-sized candy bar, instead of the little ones. Louis chuckled to himself as he decided to stop at the nearest 7-Eleven and pick up a Three Musketeers. For old time's sake.

Paul adjusted his backpack, unbalanced by the weight of the candy he'd collected. "Good stash, huh?"

Johnny smiled, an eye-liner-blackened tooth conspicuous in his grin. "Better be. This is it, you know—the last Halloween."

"Don't remind me."

"Gotta grow up sometime, you know. You'd look a little funny with a bag in your hand, going trick-or-treating when you're fifty."

Paul unwrapped a Sky bar and bit into it. "I'm gonna

really miss this," he sighed. "Sometimes I wish I didn't have to grow up."

"Don't be stupid. Anyway, there's more exciting things to do when you get older."

"Yeah? How do you know, wise guy?"

" 'Cause Vic told me, dipshit."

Paul bristled at the name of Johnny's teenage friend. "What does he know? He's just a delinquent."

"You sound like my Mom and Dad. Vic's okay."

The two boys rounded the corner to Johnny's house. Paul brightened at the thought of Johnny's mother. He'd never admitted it to his best friend, but he had kind of a crush on Mrs. Richardson ever since he'd seen *Klute* on TV. It was way cool to have a mother who looked like Jane Fonda!

Paul realized that Johnny had been talking. "What?"

"I said, 'All deaf people are homos!' Wake up!" He pushed at his friend's shoulder playfully and Paul's shoulder bag tilted, spilling multicolored candy bars on the Richardsons' front porch. Paul muttered, "Shit," stooped down, and picked up the candies.

"I *said,* I have a surprise for you! It's in the basement!"

Paul smiled and followed his friend into his home, down the hallway past the den, and downstairs to the cellar, which served as a playroom for Johnny.

The two boys spread their treats in separate piles on the carpeting. Their eyes flashed to each other's collections, checking to make sure they matched. Cheryl Richardson entered the room with two steaming mugs of cider.

"Sleeping bags are in the laundry room, Johnny. Just don't make too much noise, and promise me you'll hit the sack after the *Scream Show*. Okay?" As she set down the mugs, Paul unabashedly admired the cleavage on display from her loose blouse. He felt a by-now familiar sensation in the pit of his groin. He'd discovered masturbation two months ago in the shower and had been practicing techniques almost nightly ever since.

He watched her disappear up the stairs and shut the door behind her. Johnny yelled, giving Paul a start.

"We're missing the *Scream Show*!" He flicked a switch on the TV set. Paul turned out the lights as the voice of the program host faded up.

". . . Ghoul evening, ghosts and goblins! Now that you've gone trick-or-treating, you're in the perfect mood for tonight's scream treat. I hand-picked it from my crypt of terror!" Johnny smiled as he thought, "So did I!"

The hollow-cheeked host droned on while the two boys laughed and ate their candy bars. Finally, the film began. Johnny squealed in delight as the title flashed on the screen: *Invaders From Mars!*

"A classic!" Johnny exclaimed as he dipped a Hershey bar into his apple cider. It came up a gloopy mess, which he shoved into his mouth happily.

"I've seen this a million times," Paul complained sullenly. "Let's turn it off and read comics or something."

Johnny's eyes flashed. "Not tonight, buddy. Not on . . . the last Halloween!" He imitated the program host's weird laugh as he switched off the TV set. "Let's play a little game."

"We're not gonna spy on your sister in the bathroom again, are we? Last time we almost got caught. I thought I was gonna have a heart attack!"

Johnny lit a candle and held it under his chin, lighting his face eerily. "We're going to play Dead Man!"

"That's a kid's game."

"Not the way I play it," Johnny's wicked grin was accentuated by the candlelight beneath his face.

Paul sighed. "Okay, you got the stage."

Johnny settled back into a frayed but comfortable-looking couch. "First, I have to tell you a story." Paul groaned, which Johnny ignored.

"The story of what happened to the axe murderer."

Paul frowned. "Hey, if you're gonna make fun of dead people, I'm not gonna listen. That's sick, Johnny."

His friend clucked his tongue. "Just listen for a minute. They never found the guy who did it, right?"

"So?"

"So I know who did it."

"Cut the crap, Johnny."

"Just listen." Johnny set the candle on an end table beside him. The flickering light cast dancing shadows into the corners of the room. If Paul squinted, it almost looked like things were moving just beyond his vision. He shivered, acutely aware of how easily he had always been able to scare himself. Lately, he'd even found it hard to watch the tame horror films on TV. They made him feel . . . uncomfortable, like his drowning nightmare. He hadn't told his father that tonight wasn't the first time he'd had the dream.

Johnny continued. "The night after Vic's mom and dad got offed, I was up late reading, and I heard a noise outside the window. I turned off my light and listened. Sure enough, someone was out there, trying to get in! I *knew* it was the axe murderer, coming back to finish his work—he had to kill my parents, because they were at the party."

"Why?"

"How should I know? Do I have the mind of an axe murderer?"

Paul shrugged as Johnny continued. "I hid under my covers but lifted them just enough to see out. Pretty soon the window slid up, and saw big feet coming through the window, then legs, then a hand, and then a big bloody . . . *axe*," he screamed.

Paul jumped. Johnny grinned—Paul was so easy to scare! "I could hear this guy breathing real hard, but I couldn't see him. I figured he was right over my bed, and that any minute I was gonna get chopped in two!"

"You're sick, Johnny."

"Shhh. Next thing, he started whispering at me! 'I know you're in that bed, boy!' I was shivering so hard the mattress was shaking!

"Then he said, 'I'm gonna have to kill you now, boy. And then I'm gonna walk down the hall and kill your sister, and then your mom and dad. Now you just lay still and I'll try and get your head in one clean slice!'"

Paul could see the scene quite clearly in his mind, and he was genuinely scared—not by the game, but by Johnny. What was wrong with him lately? He was into all this weird, depraved stuff. He was harder to like all the time, which depressed Paul, who'd felt he'd always be friends with Johnny.

"I don't think I like this game," Paul complained.

"I'm almost done. Anyway, I was ready to piss my pants. But when he said he was gonna kill Mom and Dad, it made me mad . . . real mad. And brave, too. I knew I hadda try to save them.

"So I brought up my hands and poked the guy in the balls! He dropped the axe and grabbed his crotch. I got the axe and swung it real hard, *right into his face!* Well, that axe went clean through the guy's face—sliced it right in two before he could say a word! I started screaming and Mom and Dad came arunnin'. Boy, did they freak!

"Anyway, we were all too scared to call the police. So we hauled the guy's body down to the cellar, and it's been here ever since!"

"Bullshit."

"Oh yeah? Well, he's *right behind you!*"

Paul jumped to his feet. "Johnny, not only are you a fool, you're a sick fool to make up that kind of story."

"I didn't think you'd believe me," Johnny said as he rose. "But I have proof." He walked to a door on a darkened side of the room. "Wait here a minute."

He disappeared into the adjacent room, taking the only candle, leaving the room in total darkness. Paul's eyes, in a vain attempt to pull light into the room, formed colored patterns out of the darkness.

Suddenly Johnny reappeared and the room brightened. He placed the candle on a stereo speaker and started hauling some shoeboxes out of the room behind him.

"What are you doing?" Paul croaked.

"See, the only way we could hide the killer down here was to keep him in the freezer. But he was too big to fit. So we had to cut him up in little pieces."

Paul stared at the row of shoe boxes, each neatly labeled. "Eyes." "Fingers." "Brain."

Paul shook his head. "I don't want to play your dumb game."

Johnny ignored him. "The object is to touch all the

body parts in these boxes without chickening out. Whoever loses has to give the other person all his Halloween candy! Every last piece!''

Paul looked at the mound of candy that lay spread across the carpet. It was a dumb game but there was no way he could lose. It would mean lots of trips to the dentist, but he'd worry about that later.

"Okay, okay. I'll play.''

"All right! Now close your eyes and pick a box.'' Paul touched one of the shoe boxes. He opened his eyes and saw he'd chosen the one marked "Brain.''

Johnny held the box just above Paul's line of sight and opened the cover. Johnny slipped his hand inside, wiggled it around, and brought it out. "Your turn.''

Paul extended a slightly shaking hand into the box. Something slimy and stringy parted at his touch.

"Gross!'' he yelled as he pulled his hand back. Johnny grinned and he shut the lid on a box full of day-old spaghetti. Johnny chose next: the box labeled "Tongue.'' He stuck his hand inside. "Your turn now.''

Paul stuck out his hand, shoved it in the box, and groaned as he felt something long and squishy. Johnny pulled the box away before his friend saw the peeled banana.

The box labeled "Eyes'' came next. As Paul stuck out his hands, Johnny changed the rules and dumped two round blobs into Paul's hands. Reflexively, Paul's hands closed around the objects, squishing them. He flung them from his hands in disgust.

Johnny picked up the remains of the peeled plums and put them back into the box. "Just one more box, Paul.'' He held out the box labeled "Fingers'' and flipped off the lid. Johnny reached in, grabbed the withered finger he'd broken off the corpse the night before, and threw it at Paul. The boy jumped back and the digit thudded against the floor.

"You lose,'' Johnny taunted.

"Where'd you get that, Johnny?'' He'd known the other body parts were clever fakes, but this one sure looked real.

"Never mind that. You gonna touch it or what?'' Johnny started to gather up Paul's candy and move it to his pile.

"Wait a minute." What the hell, the finger had to be one of those fakes you buy in any toy store's magic department. He reached out and touched it.

Paul's body went into spasms as if he'd been hit by lightning. He was blinded, his eyeballs rolling under their lids toward the top of his head. His mouth dribbled spit as he tried in vain to yell for help. Johnny laughed hysterically at his friend's show of fear.

Paul arched back at a painful angle and dropped backward to the carpet, arms and legs flailing. Sweat poured down his brow as his eyes refocused, but not on his friend. Johnny huddled over him, suddenly full of fear.

"Paul, c'mon, it was just a gag! Give me a break!"

A voice that was not Paul's struggled out of the boy's throat. "Buried alive," it said, over and over again.

Johnny's eyes bulged. This was scarier than any book or movie. Just then, Paul's hand twitched spasmodically and the clutched finger came loose, rolling across the carpeting.

Paul's body went limp. Johnny shook his friend frantically by the shoulders and received no response. "Paul, I'm sorry! Wake up! Paul!"

This was it! He was really gonna catch hell now. What the hell had he been thinking, pulling a crazy stunt like this on his best buddy? Johnny ran up the stairs two at a time, yelling for help.

Chapter Five

The next face Paul saw was his mother's. She smiled bravely, placing a soft hand on his cheek.

"Hi, honey." Her voice was shaken by emotion.

"Hi, Mom." His own voice was barely above a croak. He looked around and saw the sterile atmosphere of a hospital room.

"Where am I?"

His father rushed to his side from a metal chair opposite the bed. "Hospital emergency room. Not a very homey-looking place, huh?"

Paul rubbed his eyes. "I just had the weirdest dream. . ."

"Can you remember what happened, Sparky?"

"I just remember falling asleep at Johnny's house. What happened?"

"We were hoping you could tell us, dear," Virginia said.

Louis interrupted. "Your 'friend,' Johnny, was trying to scare you, and I think he succeeded too well. I think you should start looking for some new friends, Paul. Johnny's not all there, if you ask me."

But Paul wasn't listening to his father's advice. In a rush, the experience came back to him like an incredibly vivid dream: An old man, dressed in a tuxedo, lying on a cushion of silk, beating his hands on an oaken ceiling just inches from his panicked, sweat-soaked face. The man was screaming that he wasn't dead, that he'd been buried alive.

Paul felt the man's loss of breath, felt his awful panic

33

and then the terrible smell as he realized the man had lost control of his bowels. The man continued screaming, and Paul could see blood dripping into the man's eyes from fingernails shredded against the unyielding wood.

His father's voice broke into his nightmarish thoughts. ". . . doctor ran a whole series of tests, and says you were just fine. Blood sugar level was a bit high . . . how much candy did you eat that night, anyway?'' Louis joked with his son, but Paul could see fear behind those brown eyes. He shivered.

Johnny quickly shoved the shoe box under his bed when he heard the knock at his door. Johnny's father walked into the room and shut the door. He was carrying a toothbrush, wearing his red knee-length robe that Johnny's mom had helped him pick out as a Christmas present for his dad last year.

"Paul's dad just called," Robert Richardson started slowly. "They're bringing him home from the hospital. He's going to be fine." Johnny nodded slowly, afraid to speak. He knew his father was really pissed.

"You still haven't really told me what happened," Richardson said.

Johnny shrugged. "We were swapping spooky stories and I guess I just kind of freaked Paul out.''

His father grimaced. "That's not good enough, Johnny. Something scared the hell out of Paul, and I want to know what it was." Richardson slapped the toothbrush against the palm of his free hand.

"Until you explain yourself, you're staying in your room. No TV, no records, no visitors." He looked around his son's room, at the Revell movie monster model kits, at the bookshelves bursting with horror comics and books, at the wall pin-up photos of weird creatures from movies.

He stood up and walked to a life-sized cartoon poster of Frankenstein, taped to the back of Johnny's door. Without warning, he grabbed a corner of the poster in one hand and pulled it down, tearing it in two. Johnny gasped. His father dropped the wadded paper and moved to another wall, where he tore down a black-and-white photo of the creature from the Black Lagoon.

"Your mother feels that you haven't had enough supervision lately." Robert Richardson approached his son's bookshelves. "Well, looking around this room, maybe I'd have to agree with her." He picked up a copy of *Famous Monsters* magazine, opened it up, and pulled his hands apart, ripping the magazine in two. Johnny blinked in amazed anger. He felt a tear well up in the corner of an eye.

In a daze, he heard his father's voice. "You used to collect baseball cards and stamps. I don't know why you like this kind of junk, but from today on, I don't want to see any of it in this house." He picked up the remaining stack of magazines and tossed them in a wastepaper basket. "I should have done this a long time ago," he continued as he shot baskets using his son's horror paperbacks as the balls and the wastepaper basket as his target. He was enjoying himself.

Johnny made a dive for the wastebasket and his father caught him roughly by an arm. "I'm serious. That's it for this trash."

"Dad, please . . . don't throw away my books." But Johnny saw something flash through his father's eyes that made him shut up. The man was really on the rampage!

"I'm not going to throw away anything," he said. "Come with me." He picked up the wastebasket with one hand and pulled Johnny along with the other. The two moved downstairs into the home's spacious living room.

Johnny's eyes bulged when he saw the fireplace and realized what his father had in mind. The man was already overturning the contents of the wastebasket onto a small pile of logs. From the stairs, Johnny's sister Annette watched the proceedings with one hand over her mouth.

"Dad—no," she begged.

Robert ignored her, turning to face his son. "It's for your own good, Johnny." He reached for the matches on the fireplace mantel.

"Mom won't like this," Johnny said. "You wouldn't do this if she was here."

"Your mother has been too lenient with you for years. If I hadn't listened to her all this time, this might never have happened. You might have been a nice, normal kid, out playing ball or riding bikes or something." He lit a match. "Maybe it's not too late for you to become the boy I always wanted you to be. Maybe someday you'll understand why I'm doing this. Maybe someday you'll thank me."

Johnny held his breath. His father let the match drop onto a *Strange Tales* comic book. The paper hissed, smoked, and quickly caught fire. In less than a minute, the fireplace was awash in a sea of flames.

Johnny stood there, hands curled into tight fists, tears evaporating from the intense heat of the blaze. His father watched the fire for a moment, then stalked away.

Johnny watched the fire until his precious collection was just a pile of smoldering ashes. His sister Annette came to his side, her hair in curlers, her feet in huge furry slippers. She put an arm around him.

"I'm sorry, Johnny."

The boy pulled away from his sister's grasp and ran upstairs to his bedroom.

Chapter Six

Robert Richardson slid the browned pancakes off the Teflon frying pan and onto a warm plate. He approached Cheryl from behind and kissed her on the back of her neck as she read the morning newspaper. She moved away from his touch.

He pretended not to notice as he dumped a stack of cakes onto her plate. She held up a restraining hand.

"Not hungry today, honey?"

"Not till after you and I talk."

Here we go, Robert thought as he placed the rest of the pancakes in front of himself and sat down.

"You spoke with Johnny," he guessed as he poured syrup from Aunt Jemima's head onto a stack of steaming whole-wheat hotcakes.

Cheryl shook her head. "When I got home from the PTA meeting, Annette was still up. She told me about your little temper tantrum. I tried to speak with Johnny, but his door was locked and he wouldn't answer me."

Robert bit into a pancake and smiled. "Yum. Sure you won't have one?"

She shook her head. "You know how much that stuff meant to Johnny."

Robert pointed a fork at her. "It was junk, Cheryl. Blood and guts crap. I tell you, the boy is on a downhill slide and I'm going to stop it and you're not going to stop me."

Cheryl's face turned bright red. "Johnny's just a teenager. He's testing his wings. It's you I'm worried about. You haven't been yourself ever since . . . well, ever since the Filippo murders.''

Robert winced, as the memory of Christina Filippo's naked body in his embrace flew through his thoughts. Did Cheryl know about his little indiscretion? Well, the hell with her if she did. What did it matter, now that the Filippo bitch was dead?

"I think Johnny needs some professional help," Robert announced. "I'm thinking of sending him to Dr. Sanders."

Under her breath, Cheryl muttered, "You're the one who needs help."

Robert slammed his fork down on the table. "What?"

Cheryl gave her husband a charming smile. "I said, pass the pancakes."

It was Wednesday, the day old Mr. Earl got in the week's shipment of comic books at Earl's Drugs. And as usual, Johnny was waiting for the codger to finish putting them on the racks. Whenever Earl bent over the comics racks, Johnny faked fart noises, much to the embarrassment of Paul, who stood nearby, munching on a Sky bar.

"I thought your dad said you couldn't buy comics anymore."

"My dad won't know what I do if I keep them hidden . . . unless *someone* tells him." He cast an accusatory glance at Paul before starting to grab the comic books he needed for the week. "Anyway, look who's talking: I thought you said your dad told you not to hang around with me anymore."

Paul grinned sheepishly and shrugged. "You know you're my best buddy—even if you did play that trick on me."

Johnny paid for the stack of comics at the front counter and pocketed a Mars bar when the salesperson's attention was diverted. Johnny winked conspiratorially at Paul as the two left the store.

As he shoved the Mars bar into his mouth, Johnny laughed and said, "You really looked weird, there on the floor, having a spaz attack."

Paul bristled. "That was nothing to laugh about."

"So what *really* happened?"

"I still don't now. At first I thought I was dreaming, or watching a movie on TV or something. There was this guy in a coffin, but he was still alive and trying to get out. Johnny, it was so real I just *knew* it was happening . . . or that it *had* happened, at some time to someone."

"Weird," Johnny whispered as he tossed the candy-bar wrapper onto the sidewalk. "Maybe somebody spiked one of your Halloween candies with LSD!"

Paul shrugged. "I dunno." He thought for a second. "Johnny, where did you get that finger?"

Johnny's face turned red and he looked away from his friend. It seemed like his entire life had gone down the toilet since the night he'd played grave robber for some stupid practical joke. He took a deep breath and launched into the story. When he finished, Paul looked at him incredulously.

"Jesus, Johnny, that's really sick!"

"It was just a joke, okay? Just a fucking joke. I thought you'd be able to handle it." The two walked along in silence for a while, finishing their candy bars.

Paul broke the silence. "I want that finger."

"No fuckin' way. After all I went through to get it . . . and after all the shit my dad gave me about scaring you. That finger is *mine*."

"I just want to borrow it for a day or so."

"Why?"

"I . . . don't know, really. I just want to . . try something."

Johnny hesitated. "If you wreck it . . ."

"Honest, Johnny, I just want to see it for a while. Maybe it'll help me to make sense of that dream I had."

"Okay, but only if I'm there. I don't trust you."

Paul scowled. Finally he said, "You're on."

Chapter Seven

Cheryl Richardson was making dinner when she heard the front door open and the sound of running feet. Seconds later, Johnny and Paul jogged past the kitchen. Surprised to see Paul and Johnny together, she followed them to her son's room.

"Hi, Paul," she greeted him. "How are you feeling?"

"Fine, Mrs. Richardson," Paul blushed.

"Your mom know you're here?"

"Uh . . . well, not exactly. But you won't tell, will you?"

Cheryl smiled and winked at Paul. She was pleased to see Paul and Johnny back together; the Silver boy was a good influence on their own son, particularly compared to Johnny's other friends, an older group of high school students who Cheryl suspected were all drug pushers.

"Hot chocolate, you guys?" she asked.

"Not now, Ma. We're busy."

"Oh. Excuse me!" She laughed and turned to leave.

Johnny shut the door and locked it. He dropped to his hands and knees and fumbled under the bed, bringing out a beat-up shoe box that Paul recognized immediately. It was still labeled "Fingers."

Johnny handed the box to Paul, who accepted it as gingerly as if it contained explosives. He set it down on the bed, and stared at the box as if expecting the finger to open the box from inside and pop out by itself.

"C'mon, already. What are you waiting for?"

"I . . . don't know. What if . . . it happens again? You don't understand . . . how it felt." Taking a deep breath, Paul grabbed the lid and threw it aside. The withered digit inside looked somehow more obscene in the light of day. Paul shook his head.

"I don't think I can."

"Don't be a jerk, Paul. Go for it."

Paul closed his eyes, gritted his teeth, and picked up the finger. Immediately, he felt a dizzy spell coming on, but much less severe this time. Feeling more in control, he allowed himself to succumb to the weird sensations.

"Are you okay?" Already, Johnny's voice sounded like it was coming from the opposite end of a long tunnel. And, though Paul's eyes were closed, an image was starting to take shape somewhere in his mind's eye. It was that damned coffin again. And the tortured man inside, taking his final breath.

Paul shivered as he watched the old man's form seemingly flow through the coffin lid and then up, through the rafters of the crypt. A full moon lit the sky as the body drifted skyward.

Johnny heard footsteps climbing the stairs. It was his mom with the damned hot chocolate! He had to awaken Paul immediately, no matter what the consequences. He shook the boy, eliciting a low moan. His mom was knocking at the door.

"Johnny? Open the door for me. My hands are full."

"I don't want the hot chocolate, Mom. I already told you."

"Johnny, don't be fresh. Maybe your friend does. Paul?"

Acting on impulse, Johnny slapped Paul's hand and the finger went flying across the room, hitting the far wall and landing behind a dresser.

Paul's eyes blinked open groggily.

"Get it together fast," Johnny whispered. "My mom's here."

Johnny jumped to his feet and walked to the door. With a cautious eye on Paul, he unlocked the door slowly and opened it a few inches.

"C'mon, Johnny. Open up. What's going on in there,

anyway?'' She peeked beyond Johnny to see Paul, stretched out on the bed. Her heart began to race. She pulled at Johnny's shirtsleeve.

"If you two are doing drugs, your father will kill you." She turned to Paul.

"Are you all right?"

Johnny held his breath until Paul responded. "I'm fine—just tired."

She felt herself untense. "This should wake you up." She set the hot chocolate mugs down on Johnny's desk.

Johnny pushed her back out the door. "This is private, Ma. We're talkin'." He relocked the door behind her.

"About girls?" she said with a little laugh. After all, they were teenagers now, and both cute boys. Johnny ignored his mother's joke and turned back to Paul.

"Well? What the hell happened? You were out cold again."

Paul's eyes sparkled. "It was incredible, Johnny!" The two settled into place on the carpeted floor and faced each other, the hot chocolate forgotten.

"It was different this time," Paul began. "I could . . . control the whole thing better. It was like I'd turned on a TV in the middle of a movie, and I was seeing it through the eyes of the actor. I saw him—or me—floating through the coffin and the crypt! And I kept going upward, till you woke me up. How'd you do that, anyway?"

"I hit the finger out of your hand."

Paul stood up, remembering the hot chocolate. He grabbed both cups and passed one on to his friend. They took liberal gulps of the muddy liquid. Paul smacked his lips in approval and continued. "Johnny, that guy was dead! And there was something else . . ." He took another gulp, while his friend listened, slack-jawed by Paul's story.

"What?" Johnny whispered.

"He's . . . RIGHT BEHIND YOU!"

Johnny jumped, spilling the hot chocolate all over his pants. Unable to control himself, Paul laughed heartily.

"Gotcha back!"

Johnny's face darkened, then regained its natural color. He started laughing, too, and soon the two boys were rolling on the floor uncontrollably. It felt great to laugh again.

Johnny struggled to catch his breath as he asked, "Was it all just a gag, Paul? Like Dead Man?"

Paul smiled and slowly shook his head. Johnny stood up, got a towel from the adjoining bathroom, and started soaking up the chocolate stains on the carpeting. He looked up at his friend, his face once again serious.

"Paul?"

"Hmm?"

"Do you really believe in life after death?"

Paul looked away for a moment, then back to his friend. "I never did—until now."

Chapter Eight

Paul picked at the fried chicken breasts on his plate, his mind on his incredible experiences that afternoon at Johnny's.

"Anything wrong?" his dad asked.

It took Paul a moment to realize his father was talking to him. "Uh-uh. I was just thinkin' . . ."

"Quarter for your thoughts . . . that's inflation for you."

Without hesitation, Paul responded, "Do you guys believe in life after death?"

Virginia nearly dropped her fork. "Where did that come from?"

Paul shrugged. "I was just wondering."

His mother put down her fork and knife. "Well, yes, Paul, I do believe the soul is eternal."

"Really?" Louis asked snidely. Ginny gave her husband a quizzical, hurt glance.

Paul interrupted. "What do you believe, Dad?"

Louis considered the question for a moment. "Well, no one really knows, son. I'm sure I don't, and I doubt your mother does, either—unless she has a hotline to heaven."

Ginny blinked; the remark stung. "I beg your pardon, Lou. My mother and father were strong believers in the afterlife, and I agree with what they taught me."

Louis shook his head. "Your parents were a bit . . . uneducated, weren't they?" He regretted the remark the moment it left his lips. Ginny had always been sensitive to the fact that, as Russian Jewish immigrants, her parents had never attended school.

She retaliated. "They didn't need a TV weatherman to tell them whether it was going to rain the next day. They could *feel* it in their bones. They didn't need modern-day medicines to cure illnesses when they grew herbs and roots. They didn't need *Time* magazine to tell them God was dead when the Torah told them that He was all around them and that, when they died, He would be there to reclaim them." She paused, out of breath.

Paul, who'd watched the exchange in rapt fascination, asked, "Mom, where do you think dead people go?"

"That's enough for now, Paul," his father interrupted. "This discussion is at an end until your mother and I have a long talk." He rose from the table and gave Virginia a "don't argue" glare. She ignored it.

"Paul, I believe there is a real heaven and there is a real hell . . ."

"You want to know what *I* think?" Louis yelled. "When someone dies, that's it. Period. No heaven. No hell. No nothing. He is embalmed, buried, and, in due time, the worms and bugs eat every bit of flesh off his body until the bones fall loose in the coffin. *That's* what I think."

He stalked out of the room. Paul expelled his breath in a rush while his mother wiped tears with a napkin.

"I apologize for your father's outburst, honey," she said shakily. "I happen to believe he is wrong."

Paul looked straight into his mother's eyes. "You're right, Mom. I know it."

Paul glanced at the luminous clock dial. It was 12:15 and he could still hear them arguing in their bedroom. He pressed a pillow against his ears and turned over, trying to count sheep. But all he saw was a series of coffins, floating upward into darkness.

"That heaven and hell stuff . . it's all crap," Louis spat out as he retrieved a suit from his closet and laid the garment over the back of a Barcalounger.

Virginia furiously brushed her hair in front of a makeup-table mirror. "Why are you so adamant about this?"

Louis tried to ignore the question as he attempted to

pick a tie to match his outfit for work the next day. Finally he answered, ''It's a long story.''

Virginia looked at the clock. ''Well, we've got the rest of our lives to tell it. You want to start now?''

Louis moved the suit and tie to a doorknob and sat heavily in the chair. ''It's my mom.''

Virginia nodded. She remembered Louis mentioning that Ruth Silver had died of lung cancer when Louis was in his teens.

''She was so full of life,'' he recalled, eyes closed, head resting against the chair. ''She fought it to the very end. But on that last day, when we knew and she knew she was going to die, she called me in to her hospital room to say good-bye. I just couldn't deal with it. I begged her to communicate with me, somehow, in any way possible, after she passed away, so I would know she was okay, that she still existed . . . somewhere. She died before she could answer.''

''Oh, Lou.'' Her anger forgotten, Virginia joined her husband in the chair, sitting in his lap, arms around his neck.

He continued, voice just a whisper. ''At the funeral, I stayed behind when everyone left the gravesite. I knelt down beside that hole in the ground and started talking to her. I asked her to give me a sign that she could hear me, but of course nothing happened. I guess I got pretty crazy, yelling and screaming, pulling the flowers away from the grave and throwing them all around. Dad had to pull me away and take me home.

''When I saw the house that she'd worked so hard to keep clean and pretty, that's when the finality of it all sank in. I knew she was really gone forever, that I'd never see or speak to her again. I knew then that the whole bit about an afterlife had to be bullshit. She was under six feet of packed dirt, getting colder by the minute.

''For me, life went on. But after that day, I've never been able to believe in an afterlife.''

He fell silent, whimpering into his wife's shoulder. Later, they moved to the bed and the comfort of their bodies' shared warmth.

* * *

3:15. Paul couldn't believe he was still awake. His mind was racing like a computer gone haywire. Ever since he'd touched that damned finger, it seemed like his life had fallen apart. Now it was even affecting his parents. He closed his eyes tightly and prayed to God that everything could be normal again in his life.

Paul met Johnny the next day by the boy's locker. Johnny noticed the dark circles under his friend's eyes. "You look like a zombie from *Night of the Living Dead*."

"Where's that finger?" Paul asked.

Johnny looked around quickly. "Shhh! Why?"

"I want you to dump it. Bury it in Highland Park. Throw it in the Genessee River. Put it back in the old guy's coffin. I don't care what you do with it, but get rid of it, please, Johnny. It's been nothing but trouble—for both of us."

"What's with you?"

"It gives me the creeps, that's all."

Johnny glared at his friend. "I'll tell you what that finger gives you: it gives you *power*, Paul. The power to see beyond death. Just think . . ."

"I don't want to think about death. I want to think about baseball, movies, swimming, summer vacation. I want to think about life, Johnny." He turned to go, stopped, and turned back to face his friend. "For our friendship, Johnny. Get rid of it."

Johnny laughed at his friend's attitude. "Okay, I'll dump it. But, hey Paul, what if the power isn't in the finger at all? What if the power is in *you*? Then what will you do?"

A chill, like a December wind speeding across a grave, scurried up Paul's back.

Chapter Nine

Johnny did bury the finger, after bicycling to Durand-Eastman Park with it safely hidden in a backpack. And every time Johnny mentioned it, Paul refused to discuss it.

Besides, it was approaching the end of the school year, and there were plenty of other things to discuss when summer vacation was just around the corner.

"Klaatu *what*?" Paul asked.

"Klaatu Berada Nikto!" Johnny repeated, as the two walked home from school. "C'mon, this one is easy!"

"Is it *This Island Earth*?"

"Nope."

"*War Of The Worlds*?"

Johnny shook his head. "Give up?" Paul bobbed his head up and down.

"It's a line from *The Day The Earth Stood Still*."

"No fair, I never saw that one." A passing metallic blue '65 Mustang honked at the two boys.

"It's Vic!" Johnny yelled as he ran toward the car, now pulling to a stop ahead of them. The passenger window rolled down and a rough-hewn face poked out. "Get in," he said, smoke wafting from his mouth like from a dragon's snout.

"Cool!" Johnny screamed as he opened the passenger door and slid in. "C'mon, Paul."

The boy held back. There was something about Vic that made him uneasy. Perhaps it was just the difference in age, or Vic's cigarettes, or the tough crowd he hung out with.

Johnny coaxed Paul. "Wake up, or we're gone!"

Paul shrugged. What harm could it do to get a ride home from Vic? He climbed into the backseat. Immediately, Vic hit the gas pedal and the car screamed into the traffic lanes.

"Man, what power!" Johnny gushed. He gazed at Vic with unabashed hero worship. Paul gulped as he watched the car speed by the other autos on the street.

"Watch this!" Vic yelled over the car's muffler noise as he cut in front of an Olds Cutlass for an unannounced right turn on two squealing tires.

"Yeah!" Johnny screamed. Paul felt the Milky Way bar he'd just consumed coming back up. "I gotta get out of here," he said weakly.

Vic ignored him while Johnny regarded him with disgust. "You chickenshit."

"I think I'm gonna throw up any minute," Paul announced. As he spoke, out of the corner of an eye he saw a bright red ball bounce into the street just ahead of them. Behind the ball was a small blur of legs and feet. A boy, no more than five, was running after the ball, oblivious to the oncoming traffic on the normally quiet side street.

"Slow down!" Paul screamed.

Vic finally spotted the child and slammed on his brakes. Paul smelled the awful odor of burning rubber and his ears were tortured by the wail of screeching tires. Time somehow slowed to a crawl as Paul watched the little boy trip and fall into the path of the Mustang. The car skidded forward.

"Nooooo . . ." The scream from Vic's throat sounded like a record being played too slow. Paul felt a thud of impact against the car and saw a tiny shoe spiraling past the car.

It seemed like forever before the Mustang came to a complete stop. Paul shook his head and time slipped back into gear. Vic half fell out of the car, holding his stomach, puking. Johnny had hit his head against the cushioned dashboard and was crying.

Paul ran back up the road to the small form that lay sprawled on the pavement. The body was bent at an odd angle, little legs nearly pointing toward the bloody head. Paul knew there was nothing he could do to help the boy now, but he wanted to get the body out of the way of other oncoming cars.

He grabbed one of the boy's limp hands and his vision suddenly blurred. Paul recognized the feeling he had hoped he would never experience again. It was already too late to stop the sensations from overwhelming him.

He closed his eyes and immediately his mind was flooded with a replay of the accident; this time, from the vantage point of the victim. Paul watched helplessly as the boy kept his eyes on the rolling ball until it was too late. Then, Paul's vision exploded into a grid of geometric flashes, each flash eroding and disappearing like a film of a fireworks display running backward. He knew instinctively that it was at this point that the boy had died. Instantly, Paul felt the boy's consciousness slide out of his corporeal form and begin a slow ascent, until from above Paul could see the accident scene and even himself running toward the body on the road.

In moments, his mental image was too far above the road to see it. City streets had become part of a patchwork quilt of colors and shapes. In a breath, he was in the dark reaches of space, and still the boy's essence rushed on, past whirling clouds of stardust and cosmic gases.

Paul heard someone talking to him, but he couldn't quite make out what was being said. He strained to hear, and the voice became louder and more clear. Paul realized with a shudder where the voice was coming from.

The dead boy was trying to communicate with him!

"Is he all right?"
"Can you hear me?"
"Is he in shock?"

A small crowd had gathered around Paul and the body on the pavement. Someone lifted the corpse onto a stretcher and, as his contact with the body was broken, Paul awakened.

Someone shone a light in his eyes. He swatted it away.

"He's not in shock, officer," an elderly bearded man diagnosed as he returned the small flashlight to a brown bag.

"Can you hear me, son?" A friendly-faced police officer leaned over Paul. The boy nodded. "Are you hurt?" Paul shook his head.

"Can you tell us what happened?"

"The boy didn't see the car coming. He was following his ball into the street." He looked over to the sidewalk, at a freckle-faced teenage girl with glasses who was crying. "The baby-sitter was inside getting some water."

"How did you know that?" the man who looked like a doctor asked.

Paul ignored the question. "You have to contact his parents. They're at Wegman's, grocery shopping. Mr. Pritchard is wearing a navy-blue sweatshirt that says University of Rochester."

"Do you know the boy's parents, son?" the police officer asked. Paul shook his head. "Then how . . .?"

"He told me." Paul pointed to the white-sheeted figure, being lifted onto a stretcher by two ambulance drivers.

"Then the boy was still alive when you reached him."

Paul didn't answer.

Chapter Ten

"Paul, you're not paying attention."

The boy turned to face his father, who was seated beside him on the uncomfortable, worn couch. Paul had been absorbed in the bustle of activity in the police department offices.

An overweight man whose girth made his police uniform look more like a clown's outfit was smiling at him. For no real reason, Paul took an immediate dislike to him.

"How are you feeling, Paul?" the big man asked in a surprisingly high voice.

Paul shrugged. "I already told you, I'm fine."

"Would you mind just going over a few things for me again?"

Paul looked down at his hands. Here it comes, he thought. How much should he tell them? That he had witnessed the accident through the Pritchard boy's eyes? That he had even somehow communicated with the boy long enough to learn his name and where his parents were? Who would believe any of that?

Detective Stan Matheson interrupted his thoughts. "From where you were seated in the car, could you see the speedometer?" Paul nodded. "Was Victor Filippo going over thirty?"

"Not when he hit Russell. And anyway, it was the boy's fault. He wasn't watching where he was going." Paul closed his eyes and clearly saw the accident repeated from the boy's point of view. Russell was definitely not watching for cars when he ran to retrieve his ball. Paul opened his eyes.

"Did you see Russell coming toward the car?"

"We all did, but not in time to stop."

Matheson leaned his bulk toward Paul. "Are you sure you're not just trying to help your friend Victor . . . ?"

"He's not my friend. He gave gave me a ride home because I was with Johnny. Johnny's his friend."

"Well, the skid marks are inconclusive. That's why we need your help to determine whether Victor acted negligently as a driver."

Paul frowned in frustration. "If you don't believe me, ask Russell."

Louis Silver regarded his son as if he were a stranger. "Paul! There's no need for that kind of talk."

Matheson held up a hand. "Paul's had a shocking experience. He may not recall that Russell is dead."

"I *know* he's dead. But I . . . never mind." He heard his father groan beside him, and didn't dare to look up.

"I think that's enough for right now, lieutenant," he heard his father tell the police officer. "Obviously Paul needs some rest." Out of the corner of an eye, Paul saw the big, sweaty man nodding in agreement with his father.

Well, Paul reflected, it had been a foolish thing to say. He didn't even know how or whether he could reach the Pritchard boy again.

Matheson broke the silence with his birdlike trill. "I think your dad has the right idea. How about if I stop over tomorrow, and we'll talk some more?"

Paul shrugged and allowed his father to lead him out of the police station to their car. As they drove toward home, Louis held his silence for sometime, then asked, "I think maybe we should stop by the doctor's office on the way home, Paul."

"I'm okay, Dad. Really."

Paul stared into space, not really focusing on the passing traffic. Occasionally, his father cast a worried glance at him, but said nothing.

Virginia Silver rushed to Paul's side when he entered

the house. He brushed past her and ran upstairs. A moment later, she heard his bedroom door slam.

Louis entered the house and sat down with a whoosh of expelled air.

She greeted him with a warm hug. "Is he all right?"

"I don't know."

Chapter Eleven

Paul locked his bedroom door and sat cross-legged on his bed. He was worried. He knew his dad was really concerned about him, and about his spacey behavior since the accident.

And then there was Russell Pritchard. Paul had spoken with the boy after he'd died. It was an incredible experience that he longed to share with his parents, but they'd never ever believe him.

Unless, Paul thought, he was able to contact the dead boy again. Paul bit a fingernail absentmindedly as he replayed the accident scene in his head. He'd come in contact with Russell Pritchard when he'd touched the boy. Now, could he reach him again without making actual physical contact with the boy's body?

Paul stared out his window. He had to admit, he didn't have the faintest idea how to use this mysterious "gift" of his.

He closed his eyes and took several deep, slow breaths. If he could just calm down . . . and maybe get a clear picture of the Pritchard boy in his mind. But it was impossible to stop the flow of other images in his head: his father, looking at him like he was crazy; that fat police lieutenant, smiling so wide it made his head look like it was cut in two; Johnny's look of horror as the Mustang slid into Russell.

Russell. He had to get a clear picture of Russell. An

image formed in his mind's eye of the boy, but it was fuzzy. He was already forgetting what the kid looked like.

With a grunt, Paul rose to his feet, walked around the room. This was no good. He just didn't know how to do it. It was like asking some guy off the street to fly a jet plane. The more he thought about it, the more confused he was. Had he somehow imagined the whole episode with the Pritchard boy? No, that was impossible—he didn't know the boy or his parents before the accident. But communicating with a dead person just didn't happen to real people, especially thirteen-year-old boys entering their adolescence (just last week he'd discovered, to his horror, his first pimple).

What he really needed, Paul decided as he opened his bedroom door and headed toward the den and his parents, was to confide in someone. To let it all hang out and see what someone else thought he should do next.

Paul felt a terrible loneliness creep up on him. Why had he been granted this creepy "gift"? Would anyone in the world truly understand him, or would everyone think he was crazy?

Paul slowly descended the stairs, catching part of his parents' conversation before they noticed him.

". . . think you're wrong, Lou." Virginia stopped speaking as she saw Paul approaching. She held out her arms to the boy and he responded with a hug. Louis patted the fabric of the couch where he was seated, and Paul plopped on the weathered but comfortable piece of furniture.

"Your mom and I were just talking about our friend Dr. Sanders." Paul gulped. He knew Sanders was a shrink, and he knew what was coming. He wished he hadn't come downstairs.

"We think it might be a good idea to schedule an appointment with him," his father continued, struggling with the words. "You've had quite a shock, you know, and we thought . . ."

"*You* thought," Virginia corrected him.

Louis scratched at the back of his head nervously. "Please, Ginny, don't make this difficult." He turned to face his son. "I just felt you might have some things you would want to talk over with him. I mean the man's an expert at things like this."

"Yeah," Paul whispered. "Just look at the success he's had with Vic."

"That's not fair, Sparky. You said the accident wasn't his fault. Look, just think about it and let us know what you decide. I won't push the idea on you. Okay?"

Paul looked at his shoes. He was still terribly confused. He was scared to tell his parents about his experience with Pritchard. Maybe he would be able to speak with Dr. Sanders.

Maybe it wasn't such a bad idea at that.

Chapter Twelve

Dr. Michael Sanders's hands shook in anger as they gripped the BMW's steering wheel. A white-faced Vic Filippo sat silently beside him, one of his arms bandaged in a sling.

"Damned good thing for you that I'm well known and liked around here," Sanders yelled. "Otherwise you'd be in juvenile hall right now. If you're very goddamned lucky, I may be able to get you out of this with no more than your hand slapped and your license revoked. And a very stiff fine, which you can repay to me in the months to come."

He looked at Vic. The boy's vacant look only made Sanders more angry. "How could you let this happen, Vic? How could you repay our generosity this way?"

Vic just shook his head slowly. Sanders would never understand him. So far as Vic was concerned, the doc was a sham. He'd never listened as Vic had attempted to explain how miserable his parents had made his life. Their lack of attention, their constant fighting, their inability to show him real affection, instead showering him with presents to try and buy his love.

So Vic had looked elsewhere for approval, to his classmates. Even here, though, he was shunned. Unattractive, hulkish, even brutish-looking, he felt his classmates' immediate fear of him. Unable to break through to them, he was forced to hang out with and quickly become the leader of the school's rather undesirables. They flocked to the group he organized, The Avengers, whose illegal and immoral exploits were spoken of throughout the school halls in hushed, fearful tones.

When his parents found out their son was the leader of a pack of drug doers and drug pushers, bullies and rejects, they panicked and told him they were going to pull him out of the school and send him to a military school.

And then they went and got themselves killed. By an axe murderer. Vic smiled to himself.

He looked at his foster father, whose attention had been diverted by the traffic. Foster father—that was a laugh, Vic thought. Sanders didn't give a flying fuck about his adopted son. For a while, Vic had hoped he and Sanders would really hit it off. But soon Vic realized that he was just window dressing for Sanders, the means to an end. That fat fuck was impotent, for some reason, and the boy was certain he'd been taken in to gain Sanders the kind of respectability that having kids gave you in a family-oriented community. Worse, Vic was sure that Sanders was flaunting his adopted son to gain the confidence of parents, who might then trust Sanders to treat their problem children.

Yep, there was no doubt about it: Vic was being royally screwed, and he didn't like it, not one bit. He'd escaped one rotten life only to find himself trapped in another.

Johnny looked at his reflection in the bedroom mirror, adjusting the gauze bandage on his forehead. It was kind of neat, really, he thought: he almost looked like one of those monsters he loved watching on TV so much. As Johnny played with the bandages, his eyes focused past his mirror image and on the memory of the accident that afternoon. He slowed time in his head to the moment when he saw the little boy. Once again, he saw the ball rolling past the car, then the boy's little sneakered feet running. Then the boy's shocked expression as he saw the onrushing car. There wasn't time for fear to register on that small face. Johnny shuddered as he recalled the sound and feel of the car hitting the child's body at thirty-five miles per hour.

Johnny realized he was sweating and wiped his face with his T-shirt sleeve. With an involuntary shudder, he realized that the tragic accident had actually excited him, thrilled him beyond anything he'd ever seen on TV or read in the books and comics his asshole father had thrown in the fire.

He didn't understand this newfound feeling of almost indescribable excitement, but in that moment, he knew it was a feeling he would have to experience again.

He gazed into the reflection of his own eyes. "I'm not crazy, am I?" he whispered. "Tell me I'm not crazy." He stopped talking to listen, cocking his head a bit as if to hear better. After a moment, he smiled.

There was a knock at his door and Johnny shook himself back to reality. "Who's there?"

" 's me," Paul answered from the other side. "What are you doin', jacking off?"

Johnny bounded to the door and opened it. Paul's expression turned sour when he saw his friend's bandaged forehead. "God, Johnny, does it hurt?"

"Nah. Come on in." He grabbed his friend by the arm and pulled him in, closing the door behind him.

"I need to talk to you about that accident, and . . ."

"That was really something, wasn't it?"

"Listen, Johnny, something happened to me that day that I haven't told anyone about." His friend regarded Paul quizzically. "I was thinking of telling my folks, or maybe even the doctor who's keeping Vic. But first I wanted to try telling you."

He paused, looked at his feet. "Maybe you can tell me if I'm crazy," Paul choked. A momentary smile crossed Johnny's face, like a cloud passing over the full moon.

Paul began. "I had another one of those weird visions, when the boy died. I grabbed his hand and . . . and I could see him, above us, looking down at his own body. It was like I was in his body."

Johnny's eyes bugged

"And another thing, Johnny: I talked to him. Well, maybe talked isn't the right word. But we communicated somehow. That's how I learned his name, and where his parents were.''

"Jesus," Johnny whispered. "That's great!"

"No it isn't, Johnny. It scares me. I didn't ask for this . . . power, or whatever it is. I don't want it. I just wish I was normal again.''

Johnny sat at his desk chair, chewing softly on one of his knuckles for a moment. "Listen, Paul, you may have to get used to this. I mean, what if this . . . power doesn't go away? So why fight it? Why not learn how to use it?"

"Why?"

"Don't be stupid, Paul. You can make money off it. You can become a medium . . . you know, help people contact their dead relatives or whatever.''

"Like old Witch Hazel, you mean?" As soon as he'd said the name, Paul felt a strange tingling in his scalp. It had been years since he'd heard about Witch Hazel; he wasn't even sure if she was real or just a myth to frighten kids away from playing on the wrong side of town.

Johnny snapped his fingers. "Why didn't I think of her?"

"You mean she's real?"

"Depends. She's a real person all right . . . I've seen pictures of her. I don't know if she's a phony though."

"Well, let's find out."

Johnny's eyes lit up. Visiting a medium would be a kick in the pants whether she was genuine or not.

Incense filled the darkened room, creating swirling mists and musky smells. A single candle illuminated the circular table where an elderly, frail black woman cried out into a crumpled handkerchief. Across the table sat a presence dressed in black, only her blazing eyes clearly visible in the glow of the candle.

"Ezekiel says to tell you he misses you, and wants you to be happy," the woman in black said softly. "He wants to remind you that, with your heart condition, you must eat better.''

The wizened black woman nodded energetically. "I will, Zeke, I promise." She daubed at her red eyes with a dirty handkerchief. "Thank you, Miz Abigail."

The woman in black slowly arose, grimacing in arthritic pain. "The séance is over. You may leave your contribution in the plate by the door."

"Thank you, ma'am. Thank you." Shaking hands brought a twenty-dollar bill from an ancient change purse and placed the bill on a shiny silver plate. "Can I . . . can I come back next week?"

"Only if you promise to eat your greens," the woman smiled. Mrs. Bender shuffled out of the old house. When the door closed, Abigail Alio lifted the dark hood off her head and allowed her stringy gray hair to flow loose over bony shoulders.

Suddenly, Abigail cocked her head to one side and shut her hazel-green eyes tightly. "Ahh . . ." she whispered, standing stock-still. After a moment, she opened her eyes again and turned back to her séance room. She had to straighten up. Company was coming.

The bus had dropped them off at the end of its line, forcing Johnny and Paul to walk the final mile and a half to Witch Abigail's home.

"My feet are killing me," Johnny complained.

"You promised to go with me."

"You coward! What's the matter . . . think Abigail's gonna stuff you in her oven or something?"

"Cut it out, Johnny. It's just this neighborhood . . ." Paul looked around nervously at the run-down houses and dark, unfriendly faces of drunks, itinerants, and jobless teenagers who walked the inner city streets because they had nothing else to do.

"So we both get our nuts cut off instead of just one of us! Thanks!" Johnny fingered the switchblade knife in his pocket. His prized possession, it had been a gift from his buddy Vic.

"Anyway, we're here," Paul said in hushed tones as he pointed toward a battered Victorian home. He started to approach the weathered wooden porch but was restrained by Johnny.

"Before we go in there, I just want to make sure you know what you're doing . . ."

"What do you mean?"

"I mean, this power you have . . . I just think maybe
you should learn to develop it—control it. Then, when it
doesn't scare you to use it, think of what you could learn
from it. I mean, shit, man, you can talk to people who are
dead! Think of what they could tell you . . . about what
it's like over there."

Paul stopped to consider his friend's comments, and was
suddenly struck by the memory of a battered black-and-
white photograph that hung in his father's room. It was his
dad's mom, who'd passed away before Paul was born.
What if he could somehow reach her? It would sure make
his father proud of him. Paul slowly smiled and nodded.

"Maybe you're right."

"Shit, man, I'm always right. Why do you think you
hang around with me!"

The door in front of them squeaked noisily open, and
both boys' breath was taken away by the woman in black
who stared out at them, beckoning them forward.

"Specters," she whispered as she sat in her customary
chair across from the two boys. Paul bit a lip to keep his
teeth from chattering. This place was weirder than he'd
imagined, and so was Witch Abigail. She'd told the boys
she'd been expecting them and had even known Paul's
name. A lucky guess?

"Specters," she repeated huskily.

"I beg your pardon?" Paul asked, acutely aware of his
high voice.

"They're all around you," the woman gestured. "You
can't see them—yet, but I can. Specters—the unsettled
spirits of those who have passed on. Spirits who still crave
human contact, who have a message to pass along to a
loved one or an injustice to be righted. They are waiting
for you to give them their voice. Right, boy?" she asked,
eyes blazing directly into Paul's.

"Wh—why me?"

"You have great power, boy. Greater than you even
guess. The specters sense this and know that you can be

their conduit to the world they can no longer inhabit nor yet leave behind.''

Paul felt himself becoming dizzy. It was too much to comprehend, to believe. He suddenly wanted nothing more than to bolt from his chair and run back to the relative sanity of the world outside this musty old house. But he was rooted to the chair. The hooded woman smiled crookedly, as if guessing his thoughts.

"You have great power, but you need help in channeling it. That is why you came here.''

"Jesus,'' Johnny whispered. This was spooky!

Abigail turned her attention fully to Johnny for the first time since he'd entered the house. The smile disappeared as she seemed to look behind his eyes right into his head. Abigail returned her gaze to Paul.

"Your friend seeks to help you, but it is he who needs help.''

"Hey—wait a minute. What does that mean?'' In a huff, Johnny stood up. "Maybe we'd just better leave, Paul.''

"Yes, leave, Dark Child. The other one stays with me. He has much to learn.''

"Uh-uh,'' said Johnny. "He goes with me or I stay.''

"Go on ahead, Johnny,'' Paul said softly. "I'll be okay.''

"No. We made an agreement.''

Abigail Alio turned to face Johnny again, her blue eyes glowing. Johnny felt the room start to swim around him and steadied himself against the back of the chair. He was suddenly nauseous. If he didn't get some fresh air in a big hurry, he was gonna be sick. He backed out of the room, eyes pleading to Paul, who shook his head.

"I'm warning you, Paul. don't stay here with her—she *is* a witch!''

Abigail pointed a bony index finger at Johnny. "The Dark Child speaks the truth, but I am not the evil one. You are. I smell the devil in you. Now leave!''

Her words penetrated his brain like a dentist's drill, and Johnny bolted down the dark halls to escape the pain. He stumbled as he ran down the porch steps, and fell to a heap. The door to the house slammed itself shut behind him.

Johnny raised himself to his feet slowly, waiting for the nausea to subside. He felt foolish and embarrassed, and more, he was angry. At Witch Abigail, sure, but also at Paul, for making him look like a coward. No one did that to Johnny Richardson—not even his best friend.

But as Johnny brushed dirt from his pantlegs and started to walk away from the house, anger was overtaken by a sense of dread. "Dark Child," she'd called him. The word sent shivers up his spine. "The devil."

Johnny stuck a hand in his mouth to keep from crying out. She was right; there was something wrong with him, and she had noticed it immediately. He hadn't really felt himself since his thirteenth birthday, though it was becoming harder and harder to remember what that "self" felt like. He'd always chalked up his metamorphosis as normal to anyone entering puberty . . . until the night he was alone in the house reading and he heard *the voice*. It had spoken to him often since that terrifying night.

"Are you the devil?" Johnny shouted at the darkening sky, awaiting an answer from beyond.

Chapter Thirteen

Paul knew he was in trouble the minute he entered his house. Not only was he two hours late for dinner, but he could tell by the look on his parents' faces that they knew where he'd been. He shut the door quietly and took his seat at the dinner table, where his parents were finishing coffee and desert.

"Johnny called," his father began.

"Shit," Paul muttered.

"Why didn't you call, Paul? You know how your mother and I worry . . ."

"I . . I didn't expect to be gone this long. But I'm okay, really, see?" Playfully, he did a 360-degree turn, presenting himself to his parents. Their expressions did not lighten. Paul grimaced and looked down at the tablecloth. "I'm sorry. I lost track of time."

His mother addressed him quietly. "Paul, Johnny told us you two went to Abigail Alio's house. That's not a good section of town . . ."

"Never mind that," his father interrupted. "Johnny also told us why you went to see Ms. Alio." Paul clenched his fists under the table. Why in hell did Johnny tell them? He was really in deep shit now. He couldn't think of anything to say.

"He said you think you have some kind of power to . . . speak with the dead, and that you wanted Abigail to help you learn how to use it. What I want to know is, who's crazy, him or you?"

Paul remained silent, realizing that anything he could say would only make matters worse.

His mother took one of his hands in hers. "Paul, if there's . . . something wrong, you can tell us. Don't be afraid. We only want to help."

Paul shook his head. "You wouldn't believe me."

Louis took a deep breath. "I think we've waited long enough," he said softly. "I'm making an appointment for you, Paul, with Dr. Sanders."

"Your father told me a pretty wild story on the phone, Paul." Dr. Michael Sanders adjusted his silk tie as he led Paul into his inner office. The place smelled of leather and stale cigars. Paul sat in a plush leather chair facing a massive oak desk. An umbrella was propped against a wall dominated by a painting of ducks landing in a pond. It was pretty much what Paul had expected a psychiatrist's office to look like.

"I don't really know where to begin," the boy admitted.

"How about the beginning?"

"Well, doctor, what's wrong with my son?" Louis asked as he met with Dr. Sanders the following day.

"I'm not really certain there's anything wrong, Louis."

"Oh come on now, don't you think that harboring delusions of being able to speak with the dead is a little unusual?"

Sanders smiled ingratiatingly. "What I meant is that I'm not convinced that Paul is suffering from anything worse than mental exhaustion and some shock from the accident he witnessed."

"Well, is it something you can help him with?"

Sanders's smile remained glued on his broad face. "I intend to try."

Johnny was cleaning his switchblade when Paul slammed open his bedroom door and invaded the room.

"What the hell did you tell them for?" Paul yelled. Johnny jumped involuntarily and the point of the blade pricked the skin of an index finger.

"Son of a bitch. Look what you made me do."

"Tough shit, Johnny. I thought you were my friend. Why'd you tell my parents about Abigail?"

Johnny bristled. "Abigail? What are you—drinking buddies now?" The two stewed in silence for a moment, and then Johnny approached Paul, placing his hands on his friend's shoulder.

"Believe it or not," Johnny said, "I did it to help you, Paul. If you can't see that Abigail's nothing but a phony and a waste of your time, then there's something wrong with you. For all you know, she might even be dangerous. Probably got a cellar full of pickled kids or somethin'."

"You're wrong, Johnny. Oh, she's a real witch all right. And deep inside you know it. That's why you had to leave that day. I think she's right, Johnny—there's something wrong with you."

Johnny laughed derisively. "You claim you can talk to dead people and you're telling me I'm sick. That's rich, Paul."

"I went to see Dr. Sanders," Paul admitted softly. "He's a pretty nice guy, and he doesn't think I'm nuts. Maybe you should go . . ."

"Don't be ridiculous. Vic says Doc Sanders is nuttier than any of his patients." Johnny shook his head. "Grow up, Paul. And don't come around here again till you do."

Johnny watched Paul leave the house from his upstairs window. A part of him mourned the loss of their friendship. But he still had Vic. And the voice inside his head.

Paul sat silently, sipping the strong, dark tea Abigail had brewed for him. The woman watched him for a while, then interrupted his thoughts. "You're quiet today."

Paul carefully set the teacup down on its china plate. "I'm not supposed to be here. My dad would kill me if he knew . . ."

Abigail smiled at the boy. "Would it help if I spoke with him? I have no phone here, but we could walk to Woolworth's and use a pay phone . . ."

Paul shook his head. "Mom and Dad . . . they just don't believe that you could really be a . . ."

"A witch." She nodded. "I understand." She touched her forehead. "Young minds are open to life's mysteries, older minds shut them out."

She sighed. "Well . . . would you rather leave, then?"

Paul shook his head. "I . . . need you . . . your help. I feel like I'm going to go crazy if I don't learn more about this 'gift' of mine, as you call it. How can I control it?"

"I promise I can help, if you'll give me time and your trust."

"I will." Paul took another sip of tea and looked at Abigail.

"You are thinking of your friend, Johnny," she said.

"Wow, how did you know?"

Abigail just smiled.

"I was wondering why you called him the 'Dark Child' the other day?"

Abigail looked past Paul, into the dark corners of the house. "Everyone has an aura that matches his personality. Enlightened people can see these auras. Yours is bright white, but your friend's is eclipsed by the devil's dark form. He may mean well, but in this life cycle, Johnny's soul has already been taken."

"It all sounds so . . . weird."

"Just the same, stay away from him, Paul. He can no longer be your friend."

The two sipped their tea in silence, and then Abigail placed a withered hand on Paul's arm. "Are you ready to start learning? Learning how to open your mind? To accept the gift you have been given and become its master?"

After a moment, Paul nodded and met Abigail's gaze. He smiled at this strange, sweet sorceress who wanted nothing more than an apprentice.

Summer was incredibly busy for Paul. He mowed neighbors' lawns to make the money necessary for busfare to and from Abigail's. Neither Paul nor his parents had mentioned his visit to Abigail since that first time, and he'd agreed to see Dr. Sanders regularly, to keep them happy. So it was easy to get away to see her; he was going to get his bike fixed, or to play with one friend or another, or was headed for the library. He hated to lie to them, but he knew they'd never understand him, or believe how helpful Abigail was.

Paul was surprised to find that in Abigail he'd found his first older friend. His favorite part of his visits with her came after they'd done the exercises she'd devised to help him hone his paranormal skills. When she could see that he'd exhausted himself mentally, she would get out the plastic Baggies of herbs and spices and brew the strong tea he'd grown to enjoy. Then, over tea and homemade cookies or bread, the stories would begin, stories of Witch Hazel and her childhood.

"I was a normal child of normal parents," she began. "They were Italian immigrants who settled in New York's Little Italy. Mama made pasta noodles for one of the restaurants, and Papa worked for a moving company. He was so strong . . . I can still remember how proud I was to see him carrying a piece of heavy furniture up three flights of stairs to someone's apartment.

"I was pretty much left to myself, and so I played with my friends in the streets. The games were not so different back then: the boys played stickball instead of baseball, but the girls played house, as they do today. All we wanted were big strong husbands like our papas." Abigail fell silent for a moment, enjoying her memories.

"One day I was playing with my friend Teresa when I suddenly felt very ill . . . it was like invisible hands were crushing my head. I fell to the pavement, but instead of seeing the wet cobblestones, all I could see was Papa, pinned beneath a piano, blood pouring from his mouth. I cried out to him, and in my head I could hear him answer. He told me he loved me and not to cry.

"I came out of the trance and ran upstairs to tell Mama what had happened. We had no telephone or car so we ran the two miles to where Papa worked. By that time, they'd been informed of the moving accident that took my papa's life.

"I was thirteen years old, as you are now. This is a time of magic . . . when one is passing from youth to adolescence and is most open to the spiritual worlds—be they good or evil. For your friend Johnny, I believe the spirits were dark. For you . . .'' she smiled and took a long sip of tea. Her vision clouded as she fell back into her childhood memories.

"Mama was a religious woman," Abigail continued, "and thought my powers were a miracle. I think now that it was no miracle but a curse, for she immediately set me up as a medium. I was young, scared, and untrained . . . I had no more idea how to contact the dead than you had when you came to see me.

"After many unsuccessful attempts as a medium, we were thrown out of the building by our superstitious landlord. Mama lost her job because they thought she'd gone crazy when Papa died. We were forced to live on the streets in the dead of winter, and Mama died of pneumonia. I . . . was taken in by some kindly prostitutes. I hid my powers from them but was determined to learn how to use them, perhaps to eradicate the guilt I felt over my mother's death.

"I worked in the bordello, washing clothes and bedsheets, until I was old enough to attract the attention of some of their gentleman callers. Then I ran away and wandered from town to town, doing odd jobs, until I finally found my way here. That was forty years ago.

"It was in Rochester where I began to understand how to focus my powers and use them to my benefit. It may not be what God intended, but it was what I knew best and I have never tried to cheat anyone. Most people still think I'm a fake, which is all that has kept me from being ridden out of town on a rail. They think I'm a witch," she said, smiling playfully. "Witch Abigail, they call me. No matter."

Paul shook his head. "I still can't believe how lucky I was to find you."

Abigail laughed. "Luck had nothing to do with it. I felt you out there, Paul. Your power is like a beacon to those who can see beyond the light of everyday life. I summoned you to me."

Paul's mouth fell open.

"That beacon is very dangerous, Paul," Abigail continued. "It sheds its light indiscriminately on those who have already passed on. Even now, you may be attracting creatures of darkness to your light." She stood up, starting to clear away their dishes. "No more time to waste. There is still so much for you to learn."

"But why would you reach out to help someone you don't even know?"

Abigail smiled out of one corner of her wrinkled mouth. "I'm not as charitable as you may think. You see, I had a vision when I first felt your aura. A vision of you, saving me." She looked Paul squarely in the eyes.

"I always trust my visions," she said.

Chapter Fourteen

It was a blisteringly hot night. Paul lay atop his bedsheets, clad only in Fruit of the Loom underpants, sweating from the killer humidity. But it wasn't the night's heat that kept him awake. He was trying to come to an important decision, weighing one side against the other.

He'd been working with Abigail for over a month now, and felt reasonably confident that he had gained some control over his "gift." She'd shown him how to envision imaginary curtains on a blank, darkened screen, then to create in his imagination a series of successive colors flowing into each other on that screen. When the screen in his mind turned so white it almost hurt to look at, she told him to watch for images floating by his field of heightened inner vision. For it was then that he would have reached the altered state of consciousness where it was possible to communicate with those who had passed on.

He shivered, mindless of the heat, as he recalled the first time he'd been able to pick out a form on that screen and summon it forward to speak to him. He was shocked to see the man from his drowning nightmares, once more attempting to communicate with him. Paul had asked what he wanted, whether Paul could help him. The image started to fade as it said one word: "Murder."

"Who are you?" Paul had asked, but the image was already gone, like a faraway radio station one hears in the middle of the night for a few minutes before it fades back into the static.

That had been two weeks ago. Since then, with Abigail's nurturing, he'd made several other successful attempts to lock the auras of specters. Each time, the effort came more easily to him, the image more clear and communication more easily understood. But he'd been unable to resummon the image of the drowned man.

Paul felt by no means adept as a medium, but he couldn't control his excitement any longer. He yearned to share his secret with his parents, but feared they would think he was having a setback and just take him straight to Dr. Sanders, whom he'd finally stopped seeing last week.

He needed real proof to convince them of his power, and he knew that the best proof would be contacting his dad's mother. But it was risky—and he'd need his father's help.

Paul slowly chewed on a lip as he imagined his parents' reaction to a demonstration of his power. Though he didn't know how, he was certain it would somehow change the family's relationship forever.

When his father banged on his bedroom door at nine-thirty that Saturday morning, Paul awoke feeling like he'd just nodded off moments earlier. He remembered his plan to contact his dead grandmother, but his head was so fogged from lack of sleep that he wasn't sure he had sufficient powers of concentration.

He stayed under the shower's cold needles until he felt more awake, then quickly toweled dry, dressed, and joined his parents downstairs at the kitchen table.

"Slept late for a Saturday," his mother commented as she set a plate of scrambled eggs before Paul.

His father smiled. "Every day's a Saturday when it's summer vacation, huh, Sparky?" The boy nodded and stared at his food without enthusiasm. His mother noticed. "Are you feeling alright?"

Paul set down his fork and rubbed his eyes. "Dad . . . do you have any of Grandma's things around the house?"

"What do you mean, 'things'?"

"I don't know . . . like jewelry, or clothes, or . . ."

"There's her collection of gold plates," Virginia offered.

Before his parents could question him, Paul jumped up and retrieved one of the plates from its perch on the dining-room hutch. His mother eyed him fearfully.

"Careful with that, please."

"You know you're not allowed to play with those, Paul."

"I'm not playing, Dad." This was it. He could sense her aura already, and was confident he could summon her. He gazed at his mother first, then at his father. Would they believe him?"

"I . . . want to show you something," he started. "Please don't get mad at me or anything." He closed his eyes, nervously trying to recall the correct sequence of events necessary to bring forth his grandmother.

Virginia and Louis traded worried glances but remained silent.

"Gramma?" Paul whispered. His voice cracked, and he tried again, louder.

"Paul . . what are you doing?" his mother asked.

"I think I can . . . reach her," Paul stammered, trying to concentrate on the changing colors of the screen in his mind. It was harder than he'd hoped. His fears of failure were getting in the way; he wasn't getting a clear picture.

"What the hell is this all about?" Louis asked angrily.

Paul pressed his hands against his ears and tried to drown out his father's protests as a form began to take shape out of the whiteness of the mental screen. He smiled as he recognized his grandmother, resembling the cheerful woman in the photo in his parents' bedroom.

The woman approached Paul with outstretched arms. In a moment, he could feel her aura enfolding him as surely as if she were next to him in the real world, hugging him. It felt good. And he realized he was grinning like an idiot.

"Tell them, Gramma," he addressed the woman he'd never even known. "Tell them you're there, and that I can see you. Talk to them."

Virginia clapped a panicked hand to her mouth to stifle her cry, but Louis was less restrained. He grabbed Paul brusquely by the arm and the gold plate went flying, smashing into bits against a far wall.

Virginia screamed.

Louis slapped his son across the face with sufficient force to feel his hand smart from the impact. Paul's head flew back and the image of his grandmother vanished instantly. The boy wriggled out of his father's painful grasp and fled upstairs, leaving his parents speechless.

He locked the door and hurled himself onto his bed, whimpering softly. He must have been crazy to think they'd believe their kid conjuring up a dead person.

Paul thought of Abigail, and suddenly saw himself at her age—a white-faced, withered old crone living in a tumbledown shack on the wrong side of town, taking money from depressed widows. The thought sickened Paul. The power Abigail had helped him harness was no gift at all, but a curse.

Johnny had been right all along, Paul decided as he wiped tears into his T-shirt sleeve. But that hardly mattered now. Paul was sure he'd already lost his true best friend.

And he was right.

Chapter Fifteen

The next few weeks were a blur to Paul, as he was whisked back and forth from Dr. Sanders's office by a sullen father or a frightened mother. Nothing he could say would make them understand, so Paul had fallen into a stony silence most of the time.

He'd tried to contact Johnny by phone, to somehow make amends for the way he'd treated his friend since he'd met Abigail. But Johnny refused to come to the phone. Finally, Paul decided to visit Johnny, hoping to corner him and then explain that Johnny'd been right all along about Abigail. She was no real friend to Paul. How could she be, if she encouraged him to use a power that only alienated everyone he loved?

Paul was just rounding the corner of the street where Johnny lived when he saw the broad-backed shape of Vic Filippo not twenty feet ahead of him on a ten-speed. Paul slowed to a stop as he watched Vic turn into the driveway, where Johnny was washing his father's car.

"Vic! How you doin'?" Johnny, astonished that Vic had come to see him, dropped the soapy sponge on the concrete, splashing dirty soapsuds on Vic's white leather running shoes. Johnny's eyes widened as Vic grimaced.

"You owe me, jerk. They're brand new. The doc got 'em for me as a peace offering. He fixed things with the cops and the kid's parents. Maybe he'll give 'em free counseling." Vic's laugh was as parched as the front lawn.

Vic scowled. "Time's a' wasting. You coming, or what?"

"Where?"

Vic's smile reminded Johnny of the frozen expression he'd once seen on a dead cat he'd come upon while bike riding. "I think it's time you joined the club."

"Jesus," Johnny whispered. "The Avengers."

"Let's go. Everybody's waiting back at the house." Johnny wiped his hands on a beach towel he'd been using to dry his dad's car. He'd have to finish later. He'd been dreaming for a shot at joining the Avengers ever since he'd met Vic.

Heart pounding, Johnny ran to his garage and retrieved his bicycle. Vic was already pedaling away from his house and it took all Johnny's strength to catch up. He didn't even notice Paul, seated on a far curb next to his bike.

By the time they reached Dr. Sander's estate, Johnny was exhausted, but he didn't dare show it. Vic hopped off his bike and let it fall to the neatly manicured grass lawn.

"C'mon, squirt. Back here." Vic ran up the gently sloping hill of the long driveway and disappeared behind an eight-foot wooden fence into the backyard. Johnny ran after him and was gasping for breath as he closed the fence gate behind him.

A dozen faces were staring at him, some more familiar than others. There was Gary Gimple, who'd just been suspended for knifing a kid during a lunchtime brawl. And there was Michael Garris, the pervert of the crowd, who'd been caught last week in the girls' locker room, sneaking Polaroid shots of cheerleaders as they dressed. Over there, smoking a reefer, was Arnie Brenner, the school's biggest dope dealer.

"What's with the pint-sized peashooter, Vic?" asked a boy named Ernie Mink with a terrible acne problem.

"He's cool. We're gonna initiate him."

"An initiation!" Arnie Brenner guffawed. "If I'd'a known, I'd'a brought a barf bag."

"Shut your hole, Brenner," Vic commanded. A switchblade knife appeared in his hand, and he ran its thin point across Brenner's stubbly chin. A bubble of pus erupted as the blade crossed a pimple. Brenner stood very still until Vic lowered the knife.

The group was silent as Vic stepped up to a redwood picnic table and gouged the switchblade into its surface. Johnny felt a little nauseous, but he was also feeling the same kind of giddy excitement he'd been craving ever since the Pritchard incident.

"Let's go," Vic growled as he snapped his fingers. Mike Garris lifted a small shoe box out of a brown paper bag. As he set the box on the tabletop, Johnny noticed the box move.

Vic turned to stare at Johnny, and the young boy saw madness in those eyes. But there was no turning back now.

"Open the box," Vic said.

Johnny felt the sweat in his palms as he grabbed the box lid and lifted it slowly. What would be inside? A snake? A spider? A dead man's finger?

Abigail Alio wrapped her shawl around her shoulders and hugged herself, but could not get warm. Something was wrong. She hadn't heard from Paul in weeks, and while she didn't have a phone, she knew he would at least write to her if something had happened.

She sat at her work table and lit a thick black candle. Closing her eyes, she allowed a mental picture of Paul to dominate her mind. Silently, she called to him.

Paul dropped the comic book he'd been reading. He felt weird, kind of stuffy, like he was getting a cold. He realized with a start that he'd had this feeling before: when he was approaching Witch Hazel's house for the first time, the time she claimed she'd been "summoning" him. He had no doubt she was doing so again now, and Paul knew why. He'd skipped several afternoon sessions with her, and she was wondering what had happened to him. Well, she'd just have to go on wondering, because he sure didn't plan on seeing her again. Only now, a week after his incident trying to contact Gramma, were his parents beginning to treat him like a normal human being again.

Paul figured that his sessions with Dr. Sanders had helped them to see that he was a normal, if mixed-up kid. He'd gone out of his way to give that impression during those meetings, going so far as laughing off his séance as a spiteful practical joke. Apparently, the ruse had worked. In fact, tonight his father had mentioned that the family would be taking its annual summer vacation next week, even though Paul had been scheduled to see Dr. Sanders again that week. Maybe, if he were lucky, the sessions with Sanders were over for good. Paul hoped so . . he knew Sanders was too smart to be fooled by Paul's lies much longer.

Paul looked at the clock on his bed's headboard: 9:15. Almost bedtime. Twice in the past week, Paul's sleep had been interrupted by the dreams of the drowning man. Who was he? And why did he continue to try and break through to Paul? The boy was tempted to attempt contact while awake, but there were too many ways such an attempt could backfire on him, especially in his own home with his parents downstairs watching TV in the den.

Paul put down the comic book, closed his eyes, and clasped his hands together in prayer. Please God, he thought, take this gift from me and give it to someone older, someone more responsible, someone who can use it to everyone's benefit. I just want the life of a normal teenager! Thanks, God.

If only, he thought, prayers were answered so easily.

It was a frog! A goddamn frog, and a big one, too. It stared up at Johnny with those bug eyes and gave a "what am I doing here?" croak.

Vic shoved Johnny out of his way. "Not just anyone gets to join the Avengers, Johnny. You gotta have guts. You know what I mean by guts? Frogs got guts. Ever see 'em?"

To one side, a high-pitched giggle escaped from Gary Gimple. Vic grabbed the frog and slapped it on the table-top, belly up. With his free hand, he brought down the knife blade and sliced a thin opening in the creature's stomach. Yellowish blood flowed slowly from the opening, in which Johnny could see miniature intestines twitching.

Before the animal could move, Vic severed one of the frog's legs. Johnny's eyes bulged as he watched the appendage actually twitch its way off the table. It flopped at Vic's feet.

The frog squirmed in Vic's grasp. The knife came down again and the frog was missing its other hind leg. Vic picked it up and threw it at Arnie Brenner, yelling. "Here's your dinner, pus-face."

Vic let go of the frog and it flipped over, trying to escape. Its terrible efforts made Johnny's stomach flipflop. He wasn't ready for this, couldn't handle it, didn't know what had ever possessed him to become Vic's friend in the first place.

Johnny wanted nothing more than to turn away and find a bush behind which he could be sick, but Vic grabbed him by the shoulder with one hand, and caught the frog with the other. "Your turn," Vic whispered, handing Johnny the knife. Johnny gagged as he noticed the yellow, thick blood on its blade. The boys standing around the picnic table were enthralled by the torture scene.

Johnny looked at the frog. It lay helpless on its back, but those eyes, those goddamn eyes were somehow staring at him, as if the frog knew it was Johnny's fault that the creature was suffering through this damnation.

"What do you want me to do?" Johnny said, hearing his words slur. He'd never been drunk in his life, but wished to hell he was drunk now.

Vic sneered. "'You ever read *Alice in Wonderland*?" Johnny nodded. The knife weighed a ton in his hand.

"Then you know what to do. Right, guys?" As a chorus, the group yelled back, "Off with his head!" It was obvious they'd all gone through the same initiation.

Well, so what, it was only a dumb animal, Johnny tried to rationalize. No one will miss it. And if this was how he could get in good with Vic, well . . .

Johnny brought down the knife so hard it went through the frog's head and embedded itself in the wood beneath.

Vic let out a war cry that was joined by the others present. Neighborhood dogs wailed in response.

Johnny felt dizzy and sat heavily on one of the picnic benches. He felt boys slapping his back, ruffling his hair, vaguely heard their congratulatory remarks.

He was an Avenger now. Whatever that meant, Johnny knew it would change his life forever.

And he was right. What he didn't know was how short that life was to be.

Chapter Sixteen

Johnny ran on molasses legs down the waving maze of halls in Witch Hazel's house. As he rounded each corner, the walls behind him contracted in on themselves, as if the entire corridor were a giant intestine, pushing him inexorably toward . . . what?

His legs were screaming in exhaustion, but he forced himself to move forward before the walls collapsed on him.

Ahead of him he could see the outline of a door. Momentarily he'd entered the room. It was her kitchen, and at one end an old refrigerator hummed noisily. Behind him the walls whooshed closed. He stopped to catch his breath, tried to get his bearings. He was thirsty.

Johnny extended an arm to the handle of the fridge, pulled it toward him, and felt the cool air of the interior greet his sweat-soaked body. Though the inside light was off and Johnny couldn't see into the refrigerator, he moved his hand around inside it, searching for the feel of a bottle.

A clawed hand grabbed his, fingernails gouging deep cuts into his tender skin. He screamed and tried in vain to pull away. Incredibly, he felt himself being drawn inch by inch into the ebony depths of the refrigerator. And now he could make out the outline of the leering face of Witch Hazel, her putrid breath searing his face as she drew him toward her. She planted cracked lips against his and stuck a lizardlike forked tongue down his throat till he started to gag. With her free hand, she shut the refrigerator door. It was totally dark.

Johnny screamed and woke up. Disoriented, he looked above him at a sea of stars. Rising off the damp grass to his hands and knees, he looked round. Members of the Avengers were huddled in small groups, talking, sharing joints, or downing bottles of booze from the well-stocked Sanders wet bar. Johnny looked down at his hand and found the remains of a joint wedged between his index and middle fingers.

Someone slapped him hard across the back. Johnny winced and looked behind to see Vic grinning down at him. "Pretty strong shit, huh, squirt? Put you right out!"

Johnny grinned sheepishly, then panicked. "What time is it?"

"Relax, squirt. The doc's out at one of his parties. We got the place to ourselves till at least midnight."

Johnny, rising to shaky feet, felt the world spinning around him. He was still really out of it, but he was damned if he was going to admit to Vic that he'd never been stoned before. "I gotta go . . . it's late."

Vic's grin disappeared. "We don't allow no babies in the Avengers, squirt. Now don't make me think I made a mistake bringing you in to the group."

Johnny gulped. What time *was* it? For all he knew, his father could be out looking for him right now. He stammered, "I just gotta go, okay?"

"So go," Vic muttered as he turned away to resume a conversation with Mike Garris, who was proudly displaying some Polaroid shots of Anne Basehart, a tomato-faced junior cheerleader, somehow caught by Mike's camera in the school's shower.

"See you tomorrow, Vic," Johnny said shakily as he walked toward the gate. He was being ignored. Shit! Only an Avenger for a few hours and already he was their laughingstock.

Just as he reached the gate, he was blinded by a pair of approaching headlights. Johnny turned around, yelling, "It's Dr. Sanders!"

Pandemonium broke loose as the various Avengers hurled

bottles over the fence onto the neighboring property or stuffed lit joints down their pants pockets.

A car door slammed and footsteps approached the gate. Robert Richardson pushed his way through the entranceway.

"Jesus Christ!" Johnny whispered.

"Johnny—do you know what time it is?" his father asked angrily. He looked around at the gathered group, noting the beer bottles that had not yet been picked up. "Have you been drinking?"

Arnie Brenner's high-pitched giggle split the air. Robert turned to face the pimple-ridden boy, who shut up.

"I fail to see the humor in this situation. Getting an underage boy drunk is against the law in every state I know of."

Vic stepped between Richardson and Brenner. "He's not drunk, Mr. Richardson," he said. His own words sounded slurred.

"I wasn't born yesterday, kid. I know the smell of marijuana on someone's breath. Where's Dr. Sanders?"

"He's out, sir." Cowed, Vic avoided Richardson's hardened gaze.

"Well, he'll hear from me in the morning, you can bank on it." Richardson turned to his son, grabbed him by the collar, and pushed him toward the car. Mortally embarrassed, the boy ran to the vehicle and jumped in.

Jesus! His life was *ruined*. He'd be lucky if he didn't get his ass *killed* for this—if not by his father, then by any one of the Avengers. How the fuck had his father found out where he was?

The car door beside him slammed closed, rocking the vehicle. His father twisted the ignition key savagely and started the car. He gunned it backward down the driveway, squealing the tires across the white concrete.

As he brought the car under control and swerved into traffic, Richardson suddenly waved his right hand in a broad arc that caught Johnny full force across his left cheek. The boy's head slammed against the passenger window, cracking it. Johnny began to cry.

"Don't give me any of that crybaby bullshit," his father shouted. "Not if you're old enough to smoke dope with that filth back there." This time Johnny saw the hand coming and swerved to avoid it, which only enraged his father more.

"Let's get one thing straight. So long as you live under our roof, you're not to see any of those boys again. Understood?"

Johnny was silent. His father whacked him again and Johnny could feel a trickle of blood drip down his cheek. He felt blind hate toward his father.

When they arrived home, Johnny fled upstairs to his room, locking the door behind him, then jamming his desk chair under the doorknob in case his father tried to break the lock.

Johnny spotted a piece of paper folded and placed in the center of his bedspread. He picked it up and read the message:

> Saw you leaving with Vic. Couldn't catch you, so I caught up with your folks instead. Hey, let's talk, okay? Call me or I'll call you.   Paul

Johnny crumpled the paper in disgust and hurled it across the room. Paul! he thought—that son of a bitch!

Johnny ran his hand across his bleeding cheek and looked at his reddened fingers. It was time, Johnny figured, to live up to his name as an Avenger.

Chapter Seventeen

Johnny pretended to be asleep the next morning when his father knocked at his door. Once he hard the sounds of his father moving downstairs, Johnny slipped out of bed and cracked open his door. He overheard his father speaking with his mom about the groceries they needed to buy that morning, and momentarily they locked and left the house. When Johnny heard their car drive away, he washed up and ran barefoot to the kitchen. He poured a glass of orange juice and made a piece of toast, put on a pair of dish gloves, and went to his father's study.

Johnny turned on the electric typewriter and slipped a piece of paper into its carriage. Using two rubber-encased fingers, he typed:

To the police:
Robert Richardson, 128 Fairbourne Drive, Brighton, was having an affair with Mrs. Filippo. She wanted to end the affair and he didn't, so she threatened to tell her husband if he didn't leave her alone. Richardson killed them both because he was scared that people would find out about it and it would ruin his life. Check it out.

Johnny took the piece of paper out of the typewriter and reread the letter he'd rehearsed in his head all night. Satisfied that it said what he wanted, he addressed the envelope and sealed the letter inside.

In fifteen minutes, he'd dressed, grabbed his bike, and dropped the letter in a mail box. Whistling as he pedaled home, he thought back to the first time he'd overhead his father whispering on the phone to Mrs. Filippo. It was on a cold winter's night, when his mom was doing the dishes downstairs and Johnny was supposedly absorbed in his homework.

It wasn't long before he'd heard his dad slip and mention Mrs. Filippo by name, and not long after that when he determined that Dad was whispering because of the nature of his relationship with the wealthy married woman.

Affairs. Johnny had read enough books to know something of them. He knew they were clandestine, dangerous, and sometimes, when discovered, they erupted into violence.

After that first conversation, Johnny had made it a habit to eavesdrop on his father, and had heard many one-sided conversations with Mrs. Filippo. The last time he'd heard them talking was the night before the murders.

He'd been reading when he heard shouting from his parents' bedroom. Knowing Mom was out for the evening with some girlfriends, Johnny immediately tiptoed to the hallway where he could better hear his dad's end of the phone conversation. It sounded like Mrs. Filippo wanted to cool things off. His dad didn't want that, wasn't ready for that.

From what he could hear, Johnny guessed that Mrs. Filippo had threatened to tell all to her husband if Johnny's dad didn't leave her alone. All of a sudden his dad quieted down, and moments later, he hung up the phone. Johnny was embarrassed to hear his father quietly sobbing.

When Johnny heard about the murders, he was immediately suspicious of his father. He wouldn't put it past his old man to have killed both the Filippos in a fit of insane anger. The thought was alternately frightening and fascinating to Johnny. He'd never intended to use his information against his dad, even after he'd destroyed Johnny's precious collection of books and magazines.

But last night's embarrassing scene at Vic's was the

capper. Whether or not his father could be proven to be the Brighton axe murderer, Johnny's anonymous, untraceable note would at least screw up the man's life for a while. And that was just what Johnny wanted.

Then, he'd go after Paul.

Chapter Eighteen

Lieutenant Stan Matheson sat behind his desk, eyes focused beyond the far wall of the messy cubicle he called an office.

Finally, he returned his attention to the letter he'd just read. Another crank? Or was this one worth investigating? One thing was certain: Matheson had been taking heat from his boss for months now about his inability to crack the Brighton axe murders.

Slowly, Matheson rose to his feet, stuffing the letter in a pocket and grabbing his car keys. He figured he had nothing to lose by shaking down Richardson a little. And besides, it was a nice night for a drive.

Johnny pocketed his switchblade and ran downstairs. "Going to Paul's," he yelled as he ran out the back door toward his bicycle.

His mother smiled, happy to hear that Johnny was going to spend some time with Paul.

Johnny pedaled along, thinking of how he was going to get back at Paul for getting him in trouble with the Avengers.

Just yesterday, he'd run into Vic Filippo at the video arcade, and was crestfallen when the older boy had shoved him aside without a word. Johnny had attempted to talk to Vic but was pushed away by some other Avengers, who'd gathered around Johnny to form a human wall between him and their leader.

"That was a dumbass thing you did the other night, little shit," Arnie Brenner growled.

"Hey, it wasn't my fault. I wanna explain that to Vic."

"Vic don't wanna know from you," Arnie hissed. "Your dumbass father called the cops on us and Vic might go to jail for offering booze and dope to minors . . . us. The cops called all our parents, and we've all been grounded." Arnie leered. "Not that we let that stop us. Now buzz off." Brenner turned away.

Johnny bristled. "But it wasn't my fault. If I could just talk to Vic . . ."

Arnie Brenner glanced around, then opened his switch-blade. "Try it and you're gonna look worse than that frog, asshole. Now get out of here while you've still got your dick."

Johnny turned around and stalked out of the arcade. Things were even worse than he had thought. Now his father and Paul would have to pay—before Vic and the rest of the Avengers decided to take things out on Johnny.

It took a moment for Lieutenant Matheson's face to register with Cheryl Richardson as she answered the front door. "Lieutenant . . ."

"Matheson," the big man reminded her as he opened the screen door. "Sorry I didn't call first. I was in the area, and was wondering if your husband was in." He gave her a wide grin, unaware that there was sauerkraut stuck between his top front teeth from the hot dog he'd consumed on his way to their house.

"My . . . husband? I don't think I understand."

"Who is it, honey?" Robert Richardson joined his wife in the doorway. Matheson watched the color drain from Richardson's face as he recognized him.

"What's the problem?" he stuttered.

Matheson swatted a mosquito that had alighted on his forearm. "Getting eaten up alive out here. Do you mind. . .?" he said as he motioned himself inside. The bewildered couple gave way to the police officer's girth and closed the door behind him. Matheson found his own way to their living room and settled into Robert Richardson's favorite armchair.

Richardson cleared his throat. "Look," he said, "we were just sitting down to dinner . . ."

Matheson pretended to ignore him. "Hot as a pistol out there tonight, isn't it? I'd kill for a lemonade right now." He smirked. "Just an expression."

"I'll get some," Cheryl said as she left the room, leaving her husband standing bewildered next to the police lieutenant.

"Now, what is it you want, Lieutenant Matheson?"

"Too hot to stand on ceremony, Mr. Richardson. Why don't you sit down?"

Richardson bristled, feeling his face flush. He didn't like being ordered around in his own home. He stood his ground, remaining silent until Matheson shrugged and continued speaking.

"So tell me, Bob . . . can I call you Bob?" Richardson held his silence. "Tell me, Bob . . . how was she in bed? Mrs. Filippo, I mean."

Richardson could feel his face turning beet red. He opened his mouth to speak, shut it again, knowing that whatever he said could be held against him later in court. Finally, he stammered, "Isn't this about the time where you read me my rights?"

Matheson sneered. "Well, hell, we're just sittin' here talkin', big guy. Man-to-man-like." Matheson shifted his weight in the comfortable chair and opened a package of cigarettes without bothering to ask if Richardson objected. He lit one and continued.

"I'll tell you, Richardson. When I saw Mrs. Filippo, she wasn't looking any too attractive. Lots of blood will do that to a person—not to mention the loss of one's head. Oh, I'm sure she was pretty good for a babe her age. But really, you're pretty well set in the female department, if I may say so." He twisted his head toward the kitchen, where both men could hear ice tinkling into glasses as Cheryl fixed lemonade.

"Does your wife know about your affair with Mrs. Filippo?"

Feeling dizzy, Richardson sunk into the cushion of a couch opposite Matheson. The big cop took out a weathered notepad, flipped past several pages, then studied one.

"You know," he said slowly, "I have my notes with me from the night of the Filippo murders, and I don't see any mention from you about an affair with the deceased. I don't appreciate people holding back important information like that, Bob." He exaggerated the name as he said it, making it sound like the punchline of a bad joke.

Richardson lost control of himself, launching his body at Matheson's great bulk, sending both men tumbling backward as the chair Matheson occupied collapsed under their combined weight.

"You motherfucker," Richardson screamed as he pummeled Matheson with his fists. "You want me to confess—to make your job easy. But I never killed anyone."

Matheson was still smiling. With very little effort, he grabbed Richardson's hands and pulled them away from his face, until the man was forced off balance and fell away from the police lieutenant. Matheson rose above Richardson, who was suddenly struck with the image of the dancing hippopotamuses from the Disney film *Fantasia*. My God, he really was losing his mind! How the hell had he allowed himself to attack Matheson?

Cheryl reentered the room and screamed as she viewed the scene. The silver tray with the two glasses of lemonade she carried crashed to the carpeting. Matheson slowly pulled his big fist across his bleeding lip and gazed at the blood for a moment.

"I think you'd better come with me, Mr. Richardson." He gruffly pulled the smaller man to his feet. Richardson would not allow his gaze to meet his wife's.

"What's the charge?" Cheryl cried shrilly.

"Right now, assault and battery. By the end of the night, maybe we can add murder."

"Geez, Johnny, it's great to see you!" Paul enthused as he joined his old friend on Paul's front porch.

"Can you get out of here for a while?"

Paul looked at his watch. "Long as I'm back before dark."

"Look, you wanna settle things between us or not?"

"Sure Johnny." Paul was disappointed by his friend's gruff behavior, but he wasn't going to argue, not if it meant jeopardizing the chance to get their friendship back in gear.

"Get your bike."

"Let me tell Mom and Dad . . ."

"Fuck that. Let's just go."

Paul hesitated, then ran to the backyard, retrieved his bicycle, and hopped on. "Lead the way."

They parked their bikes under the cool shade of the tall pines that ringed the bottom of Cobb's Hill reservoir. Johnny ran ahead of Paul, following a favorite trail that led uphill to the water supply at the hill's summit.

Each time Paul attempted to catch up to Johnny, the older boy ran ahead. Finally, exhausted and disappointed, Paul stopped. "I thought you wanted to settle things," he yelled ahead into the forest. Johnny had disappeared somewhere down the trail.

Paul sat down on a nearby tree stump to catch his breath. A wisp of breeze helped cool off Paul. He could already see the sun setting between the trees. Soon he'd have to turn around and head back home or he'd catch hell from his folks.

Johnny jumped in front of him, switchblade knife catching the final rays of the sun, throwing its reflection into Paul's bulging eyes.

"Jesus, Johnny, you scared me. Where'd you get that thing?"

"Gift from Vic," Johnny growled. "That's when we were still buddies. Now he wouldn't go out of his way to shit on me."

"Why?"

"It's all your fault, dickhead," Johnny screamed, unaware that his voice had risen several octaves. "That night you came to see me, when you saw me go off with Vic—you told my dad where I went."

Paul started to disagree, but Johnny cut him off. "The old jerked walked in on my initiation into the Avengers."

"Your initiation . . ." Now his friend's behavior made more sense. The Avengers were notorious. "I . . . I didn't know," Paul offered meekly.

"That doesn't matter, asshole. The result was the same. I worked hard to get in good with Vic, and now I'm gonna have to work harder to stay out of his way." Johnny underscored his frustrated anger by lashing his knife toward Paul, who ducked back just in time to miss the sharp blade.

"Hey, watch that."

"No, you watch it, jerk-off. I figure, you got such a big mouth, maybe you'd like me to widen it for you even more. Huh?" Johnny aimed the knife at Paul's face.

"Johnny, stop it. I made a mistake and I apologized. What else can I do? Cool out!"

But Johnny lunged again, scraping Paul's cheek with the blade. Paul hissed in pain, angrily grabbing for the knife. The two boys struggled, and Paul was able to grab the weapon out of Johnny's grasp.

Suddenly, Paul felt his body grow numb. The knife clutched in a rock-hard grip, he fell to the ground. Visionary images were already crowding his mind.

In his mind's eye, he was a plushly appointed bedroom, flat on his back on a large bed. Above him a naked woman bounced up and down on his stomach. Above her, a mirror was mounted on the ceiling. Paul was horrified to recognize the faces of Vic Filippo's father and mother.

Though he'd never experienced intercourse, there was no doubt as to what the two were doing. He could smell their mixed sweat, hear their grunts, even feel the man's rushing heart beat. He heard himself say, "Oh my God, I can't wait anymore!"

And in an instant, Paul was experiencing Carlo Filippo's orgasm. Paul groaned in ecstasy, his heart racing to the point of near-collapse.

Paul "watched" as the naked woman fell into "his" arms. Then, from above her head, Paul saw another shape reflected in the mirrored ceiling. He felt Carlo's eyes bulge in surprise, a moment before he saw an axe blade descend. An instant later, he heard Mrs. Filippo's groan and saw her head fall to the side as jugular veins spurted blood from her neck into Carlo's face.

The axe blade split the flabby skin of Carlo's neck. Impossibly, Paul viewed the scene from Carlo's eyes as his head fell off the bed and hit the floor with a dull thud. The room hung at a crazy angle, bedposts and dressing table leaning drunkenly. Above him, Paul spotted Carlo's left arm and hand, flopping across the bed's edge like a beached fish.

The pain in his neck subsided as Paul felt Carlo take his final breath. The image disappeared just as the murderer came into view.

Chapter Nineteen

Johnny watched Paul writhing on the ground, the knife clenched in one wavering hand. Paul was either faking a vision or actually having one. In either case, Johnny could not retrieve his weapon. Every time he tried, Paul would jerk away, and the knife would slash through the air, inches from Johnny's fingers. Finally, Paul lay still long enough for Johnny to grasp the switchblade and pull it free.

Paul groaned and blinked his eyes open. Immediately, he turned to one side and heaved his dinner onto the ground. Finally, he wiped his mouth with his shirt-sleeve. He looked up at Johnny.

"Where did you get that knife?"

Taken aback by the incident, Johnny answered without thinking. "From Vic. He said he stole it from old man Filippo."

Paul held his stomach with one hand as he used the other to steady himself while rising to his feet.

"That's why I saw what Mr. Filippo saw when . . ." As the bloody images rushed back into his memory, he felt bile begin to rise in his throat. He clapped a restraining hand over his mouth.

"What? What are you talking about? What did you see?"

Paul shook his head. If he didn't stop thinking about it, he was going to barf again, and he already felt terrible.

Johnny shook Paul by the boy's bony shoulders. "What did you see?" he screamed.

The shaking was making him nauseous again. "I saw Mrs. and Mrs. Filippo being murdered . . . through Mr. Filippo's eyes. Johnny, it was . . . awful." Paul belched.

"Did you see who killed them?"

"Give me the knife again. I almost saw the guy's face just as I lost contact."

Johnny glanced at the knife in his hand. If Paul recontacted Filippo by touching the weapon, he would learn the murderer's identity. And if it wasn't Johnny's father, then his plot for revenge would fail. He couldn't let that happen.

Without warning, Johnny flung the knife far over his head. They both heard a splash as the knife hit the reservoir waters nearby and sank from sight.

Before Paul could voice his complaint, Johnny had mounted his bicycle and pedaled away. Paul looked at the reservoir, its water glowing in the dark of the rising full moon. It would be impossible to obtain the knife now—impossible to track down the Filippos' murderer . . . unless he had help.

He righted his bike and began the ride home. Tomorrow, he decided, it would be time to recontact Witch Hazel.

Paul had just joined his parents at the breakfast table when Cheryl Richardson called. She spoke first with Paul's mother, then his father. When Louis finally hung up, his face was drained of color.

"Pour me some more coffee, would you, Ginny? I'm gonna need it." She did so and waited for him to speak. He downed half the cup and turned to her.

"I . . . hardly know what to say."

She took his hand. "I'm sure he's innocent. I mean, he's our best friend . . ."

Louis shook his head. "I just don't know . . . he has been acting strangely."

"But why would he . . ."

Paul interrupted. "What's wrong?"

Virginia searched Louis's eyes for the proper words.

Finally she said, "It seems that Robert Richardson—Johnny's father—has been charged with murder."

A chill raced up Paul's spine. "The Filippos," he whispered.

"How did you know that?" his father asked.

"I heard you mention the name." That was a lie, but Paul hoped his parents wouldn't notice. He couldn't tell them about his vision last night. Not when they thought he was "normal," thanks to his visits to Dr. Sanders.

But had it been the face of Robert Richardson he'd seen in his vision? As hard as he tried to recall, Paul could not honestly say whose face it was he had nearly glimpsed. Now he was more determined than ever to contact Witch Hazel.

At first, she wouldn't admit him. She stood in the half-opened doorway waiting for him to explain his long absence. Paul looked down at his feet, feeling ashamed for doubting this woman.

The words came slowly as he tried to explain how his attempt to contact his grandmother had backfired. He mentioned the embarrassing visits to Dr. Sanders, who patronized the boy but obviously didn't believe a word he said. Finally, he spoke of the incident last night, culminating in the vision and the lost knife.

When his story was complete, he waited for her to speak. She chewed on her upper lip, taking her time in deciding whether to let this boy back into her life.

"You hurt me, you know," she finally said, her voice a hair above a whisper. "When you didn't come by, I even tried to contact you—here," she said as she pointed to her forehead. "You felt it, didn't you?"

Paul looked at the rotting floorboards of the porch and nodded.

"Why didn't you respond?"

"I . . . I was all screwed up. I still am." He finally looked at Abigail's withered face. "I need your help." He couldn't stop the tears. "Please."

Still she stood there. It was true he'd hurt her pride. She hadn't allowed anyone to get close to her in years, and when she had, with Paul, he'd repaid her kindness by deserting her. Would it happen again? And more—did she still care about him?

Slowly, a smile crept across her features and she opened her arms to him. He nearly leaped into them, and the two embraced.

Wiping a tear from his eye, Abigail asked, ''Want some iced tea?'' As she shut the door behind them, she picked up strange emanations from the air surrounding the house. Maybe a storm was coming.

At the end of the street, Louis Silver sat in his car, watching his son enter Witch Hazel's house. Louis's hands clenched and unclenched against the steering wheel. He couldn't believe his son had disobeyed his direct order not to visit Hazel again. Something would have to be done about his behavior.

Tomorrow, Louis would call Dr. Sanders.

Chapter Twenty

Michael Sanders was nine, and his father was beating him again. The man was using the blunt end of an umbrella to hit his child. Even now, seated in a comfortable lounge chair, reliving his memories, Sanders involuntarily lifted his arms to shield himself. Slowly, he lowered them and settled back into the recliner. He was safe, he reminded himself.

Bitterly, he recalled his father: a big, swarthy man with no educational background to speak of; a factory worker in the seamy side of town who turned most of his paychecks into liquor purchases. Joshua Sanders would return to the tiny, dilapidated apartment he called home, swaying on his feet, yelling at Michael's mother to take his shoes off, or demanding that she have sex with him right there in the living room, despite five-year-old Michael's presence. When his mother would refuse, his father would pick up the umbrella and beat her. And while those beatings always started with his mother, they always ended with Michael.

Michael was often awakened by the agonizing pain of the umbrella shaft slamming down on his small body. Michael would crawl under the bedsheets for protection, and he could still recall his father's savage snarl as he tore the sheets away from young Michael, so that he could better aim the blows.

His father had told Sanders that each beating was necessary, that Michael had been bad in some way or other and deserved to be punished. It would be years before Michael would come to doubt his father's admonitions.

As a youngster, Sanders had wondered why his apartment neighbors never responded to his screams of pain. As a grown-up, he realized ruefully that his childhood neighbors were downtrodden itinerants with problems of their own, or people too old and frightened of his father to stop the beatings, or even report them to the police.

Sanders recalled childhood fantasies that he and his mother would run way and start their life over again. But she never did, and only later, when Sanders had studied psychology, did he come to understand that the woman had been entirely cowed by her terrible marriage.

An only child, Michael turned to his school friends for the only enjoyable experiences in his young life. But he refused to speak of the beatings with them or his schoolteachers, never being quite certain that he did not actually deserve the punishments. Worse, he feared what would become of him if he did tell on his father.

But one day, his father had gone too far. He'd come home, stinking of liquor as usual and yelling about having lost his factory job over a fight with his boss. He bragged that it took half a dozen co-workers to restrain him from bludgeoning his boss to a pulpy mess with a crowbar.

His mother, normally docile during their fights, had summoned the courage to ask where their money for food and shelter would come from. She was swatted out of the drunken man's path.

Michael had watched as his mother twisted an ankle and slammed into the sharp edge of the kitchen table, the hard metal biting into her throat. Through a web of crossed fingers over his eyes, he saw blood spurt all over the room while his father grunted and then laughed, a sound that haunted Michael to this day.

It rose in his own throat, first as a cry of pain, then as a series of hoarse gulps, finally a full-blown howl. It was the laugh of madness. But his wife, Betty, was at a women's social, so Sanders let himself revel in the laughter until his sides hurt and his throat was raw.

He looked around the room. Where was Vic? Would he

hear him? He calmed himself as he recalled that Vic was out with those hoodlums he called his friends.

Sanders felt something wet and looked down to see he'd lost bladder control during his laughing jag. That was very naughty, and naughty boys had to be punished.

He went to the hall closet and grabbed the umbrella, then moved upstairs to his bedroom, where he disrobed and climbed into bed.

"Bad!" he whispered as he hit himself against the arm with the wooden umbrella shaft. He winced at the pain. A corner of his mind clung desperately to sanity, reminding him not to hit himself someplace visible to others.

"Bad!" he whispered, accentuating the word with another slap of wood against soft skin. When he felt he'd punished himself as much as his daddy would have, he let the umbrella drop to the floor. He cried into his pillowcase for a while, then struggled to regain control.

With control came the flood of memories. His father was bending over his mother, whose life was ebbing away on the kitchen floor. His father turned to face him and for the first time, the nine-year-old boy truly understood that his father was mad.

Michael ran into the living room, grabbed his father's umbrella like a lance, and ran back into the kitchen, approaching his father from behind.

The boy aimed the shaft at that broad back, but the sound of his footsteps deceived him. His father, still kneeling by his mother, turned to face his defiant son.

Michael ran the tip of the umbrella straight into his father's right eye. He saw the tip lance the soft orb and continue till it was embedded several inches in the man's head. When he fell back and struck the floor, the umbrella sagged like an uprooted tree, finally popping out, displaying the speared eye on its tip.

The apartment was silent. As usual, there were no inquiring neighbors, not even a dog barking in the building.

The boy walked slowly to his bedroom, got into bed, and drew the sheets over his head.

The police found him there, sucking his thumb, in shock. He was taken to a hospital, and later relocated to an orphanage and quickly forgotten. Life there was little better for him: too many youngsters, too little guidance. Too much punishment. No love.

So he'd turned inward, spending his free time reading. As he grew older, he found the psychology section of the local library, and devoured books that dealt with aberrant parental behavior.

It was only natural that, when Michael Sanders was old enough to leave the orphanage and start life on his own, he turned to a career in psychology. By that time, his interest in the field had been rewarded with a full scholarship at the University of Rochester.

That was twenty-five years ago. Since then, he'd specialized in working with troubled families like the Filippos, whose wealth had made them selfish and self-destructive. Sanders was especially concerned that their behavior would harm their teenaged son Vic.

Shortly after he began seeing the Filippos, Sanders requested a private session with Vic. Sanders asked whether he'd ever been beaten by his parents. Vic claimed he had not, but Sanders knew better. He yearned to tell the boy that he understood his fear of telling the truth. He knew what Vic had to be going through, and that made him angry.

That anger gave birth to the plan. Sanders decided to adopt Vic, to give him the guidance so sorely lacking in his own childhood, and now mirrored (or so he thought) by Vic's circumstances.

Of course, he couldn't adopt Vic if his parents were still in the picture. They'd have to be locked out of Vic's life— permanently.

The idea of murdering them did not strike Sanders as odd. After all, the Filippos had been bad parents and deserved to be punished. It was really that simple. And so he had punished them both, gaining a son in the process. His own wife, infertile and unaware of Sanders's role in the Filippo murders, had warned her husband that Vic was not going to be a model son. That only firmed Sanders's resolve to take in the boy.

It's true, Sanders admitted to himself as he put on a

long-sleeved silken robe, that things hadn't gone well with
Vic. The boy was stronger, more independent than Sand-
ers had been at his age. Since adopting him, Vic had
become sullen, unruly, unpredictable, even dangerous.
Worse, he had become a source of embarrassment for
Sanders.

His thoughts were interrupted by the clanging of his
business telephone. Sanders glanced at his clock. It was
late. Any patient calling at this hour was obviously in
trouble. He picked up the line.

"Michael? It's Louis."

"Is something wrong?"

"Well, I . . I don't know," Louis stammered. "It's
about Paul. He's been to see that old witch . . . Abigail
Alio again."

"I see." Sanders was certain that Paul Silver was just
another underloved child who had invented a fantasy world
because his real world provided insufficient love and attention. Sanders didn't believe for a moment all the hogwash
about Paul's supposed ability to speak with "specters," as
the boy called them. Sanders had worked with the boy for
weeks and was disappointed to hear that the sessions had
apparently not helped Paul. More drastic measures were
called for.

"Let's make an appointment for Paul to see me tomorrow, shall we?"

Louis squeezed his wife's hand. "That would be great.
Thanks so much." He hung up the phone and embraced
his wife. "Everything's going to be fine," Louis reassured
her.

Chapter Twenty-one

Paul sat cross-legged on his bed, practicing the techniques Abigail had demonstrated. He had been surprised at how much he'd lost or forgotten since he'd seen her last. She had reminded him that his gift, like any talent, would fade if not practiced. In fact, he was again unable to summon any specters without touching an object they'd once owned. Now it would surely be some time before he could hope to solve the Filippo murders.

That's why he'd decided to visit Lieutenant Matheson this morning, to make some kind of excuse and ask him for some object of theirs. Anything would do, from a key to a book. Right after breakfast, he thought, he'd hop on his bike and . . .

There was a knock at his bedroom door. He uncurled, stood up, and answered it. His father was not smiling.

"Where were you last night?"

Paul gulped. Could he dare to tell the truth?

"Never mind the lies . . . I already know." He stepped beyond Paul into the room, and sat heavily on the edge of the bed. "I don't understand, Paul. Why do you insist on seeing that woman?"

"She's lonely, Dad. And she's not so bad, really. We're kinda . . . friends."

Louis shook his head. "I won't have it. She lives in a dangerous part of town, and she puts crazy lies in your head."

"They're not crazy," Paul muttered despite himself.

Louis sighed. "Since that's the way you feel, I'm taking you back to Dr. Sanders."

"Dad, no. I'm fine. You're just wasting your money."

"That's my concern, Paul. You obviously haven't been listening to the doctor. Maybe now you will." He looked at his watch. "Better get dressed. I'm going to see if I can get you in to see him later this morning."

"Today?" There went his trip to see Lieutenant Matheson.

"I hope you didn't plan on visiting Witch Hazel today, Paul. Maybe I haven't made myself quite clear, young man. You're not to visit her ever again. Do you understand?"

Paul envisioned the murders of the Filippos. "It's important . . ."

"Why? Just tell me why . . ."

His mouth opened and closed. Would could he say? "You'd never believe me."

There was silence for a moment. "No. No, I suppose I wouldn't."

"Well, Paul, it's nice to see you again." Sanders smiled at the boy who occupied the traditional patient's chair opposite his. "Do you know why you're here?"

"Because my dad made me come."

"And why is that?"

Paul hesitated. He'd already told Sanders about his spectral visions. Why not explain the rest? He couldn't be in much worse trouble regardless of what he said. And maybe, just maybe, Sanders would believe him and even be able to help him.

So he explained his ghastly vision of the deaths of the Filippos. At first, the words came out haltingly; then, as he became immersed in the story, it was all he could do to keep from tripping over his tongue in the rush to explain what had happened and how he might be able to discover who their murderer had been. As he explained, he watched for Sanders's response, but the man was impossible to read. Sanders sat there, just listening, not interrupting him or even taking notes. When Paul was finished, the room was quiet for a moment.

"Well, Paul," Sanders said, "I hope you can understand why I find it hard to believe what you've just told me."

The boy nodded. It had been a gamble and it hadn't paid off. It figured.

Sanders could read the disappointment in Paul's face. "Tell you what. Give me the night to think this over and then let's get back together tomorrow to determine our next move. Okay?"

Again, Paul nodded. Ahead of him he could see more months of useless counseling. He stood up to leave.

"Oh . . . and Paul? Let's make that meeting tomorrow with you and your parents, all right?"

"All right."

Once the boy was gone, Sanders allowed the smile on his face to disappear. He grabbed a handkerchief from his suit pocket and wiped the sweat off his brow.

Either the kid was crazy or he was about to discover that Sanders was the Filippo killer. Either way, Sanders couldn't chance the Silver boy retelling that story to his parents or anyone else. If he did, and someone even considered his story, Sanders's fate was sealed.

There was no doubt about it—the boy had to die. And, just to make sure his parents didn't talk, they'd have to die, too.

Sanders canceled the rest of his appointments for the day. He had to determine a way to get rid of the Silver family immediately, without arousing suspicion.

He advised his secretary to cancel his appointments for the next day and to take the day off herself, explaining that he'd decided to spend the day at the university library doing research on Paul's case.

Alone in his office, he considered murder weapons.

As his father drove him home from the session, Paul remained silent. His thoughts were of Abigail. More than anything, he wanted to speak with her, get her advice, her spiritual guidance. But the woman had no telephone, and Paul knew he'd be skinned alive if he tried to make it to her side of town again.

Then he remembered the conversation he'd had with her

when she'd said that she'd attempted to contact him mentally. Telepathy was an even more foreign concept to Paul than his power to communicate with specters. But maybe, if he just thought strongly about her, she would pick up his thoughts and do the hardest part of the job for both of them.

So he sat there, ignoring his father's worried glances. He shut his eyes tightly, picturing first the street where Abigail lived, then the house, then inside the house in her parlor where they shared iced tea. Finally he focused as clearly as he could on her face, and repeated her name over and over to himself.

He felt nothing in return. It was hopeless. He felt like he was playing one of Johnny's stupid Halloween games. Maybe he really was going crazy, he thought with a shudder.

He was silent the rest of the ride home.

Abigail awoke from her catnap with a headache. Woozily, she reached for a bottle of aspirin and then realized that what she was experiencing wasn't a headache at all. She relaxed her mind and immediately an image overtook her: Paul, seated in a car. She smiled in pride at the thought that he'd been able to contact her telepathically. The boy had great power, of that she had no doubts.

What he did want? Was something wrong? Abigail got up, fixed herself an iced tea, and sat at her parlor table. When they'd last spoken, he was terribly concerned about finding out who'd killed the Filippos. Was that it? Had he been able to discover the killer's identity? Or was he having trouble and needing her help?

Abigail set the perspiring glass on the faded linen tablecloth and allowed her mind to become clear. Whatever the problem was, she wanted to help Paul.

Chapter Twenty-two

The rest of the day had been hell for Paul. His parents would barely speak to him, and when they did, it was just to ask more questions about his visits to Abigail. As Paul readied himself for bed, he decided that there was only one way to convince his parents and Dr. Sanders that he wasn't nuts: to solve the Filippo murder case.

His parents hadn't allowed him to leave the house that day, nor use the phone, so he'd been unable to reach Lieutenant Matheson. His only hope was to call upon his own resources, to try and focus his powers to call forth the specter of one of the dead Filippos. So once again he sat cross-legged on his bed, clearing his mind of any conflicting imagery until he was able to focus on a screen that changed colors from dark to light to blinding bright white.

Mentally, he called on Carlo Filippo to appear before him, unaware that Abigail Alio had already spoken to the specter of the murdered man.

Hazel had to calm herself or she knew she would lose control. She made some more iced tea, hands shaking as she poured the liquid into a tall glass.

My God! she thought as she sat at her table. My God! It was Sanders, the doctor Paul had described so many times to her.

With some effort, she'd been able to contact the specter of Carlo Filippo, still wandering aimlessly between psychic planes, a tortured soul torn from life before his time, clinging to his earthbound roots.

She'd seen his murder through his anguished eyes and had elicited from Filippo the name of his murderer.

And now that she knew it was Sanders, she had to alert Paul and the police without delay. For hadn't the boy been seeing Sanders throughout the summer? Who knows what he'd said to the doctor already that could endanger his life.

She cursed herself for not being able to afford a telephone. Well, no matter, she thought as she gathered up her change purse. It was late . . . Woolworth's, with its pay phone, would be closed. But she would pound on neighbors' doors or walk till she found a phone booth. First, she'd call Paul, then the police.

What would she tell them? They'd think she was crazy. No matter. No matter how she claimed to have found out about Sanders, they'd have to investigate her story. Wouldn't they?

At midnight, Paul quit, admitting to himself that he was just too tired to concentrate. Perhaps he was just trying too hard. In any case, he'd been unable to summon any specters, so he turned in, vowing to try again the next morning.

When the phone rang in the Silver home, Paul was dead to its sound.

Surprised out of a sound sleep, Louis cursed and reached for the receiver, knocking it off its cradle and onto the carpet. He groped for it in the dark and finally found it.

"Hello?" Through bleary eyes, he saw the time on the bedside clock: 12:13.

"Paul is crazy," a voice whispered back to him. "He ought to be in a nuthouse."

"Who is this?"

He was answered with a dial tone.

Virginia stirred. "Who is that?"

"Crank call."

"What did they say?"

"It's not important. Go back to sleep."

Troubled, Louis replaced the receiver in its cradle and stared at the ceiling. He wasn't able to place the voice, but why would anyone say something like that about his son?

The phone rang again. Irate, Louis reached over, lifted

the phone off its hook, clicked the plunger till he heard a dial tone, then buried the receiver inside the top drawer of the nightstand. He wouldn't stand for being awakened throughout the night by some jerk who had nothing better to do than bother people.

Abigail heard the phone being answered, but before she could say one word, she was cut off and heard a dial tone. She dialed the number again but got a busy signal, tried a third time five minutes later and heard the same tone. Frustrated, she dialed the Brighton police department.

In his bedroom, Johnny Richardson giggled into his pillowcase. If Paul Silver thought he was done with him, he had another think coming. Now that Johnny's father was being questioned for the murder of the Filippos, Johnny couldn't allow Paul to testify that he'd ''seen'' the Filippos die in one of his spectral visions. Johnny had to make sure that no one would listen to him, and a series of crank calls to Paul's parents was just the opening salvo in his war against Paul.

Johnny was unaware that his thoughts were no longer his own, that he was under the control of something less than human.

At the Brighton police department, Sergeant Bronstein picked up the phone, surprise barely contained in his voice. There was never an overnight emergency in Brighton. The town had been deadly quiet since . . . well, ever since the Filippo murders.

"May I have . . . the person investigating the Brighton axe murders, please?" Abigail asked in a halting tone.

Bronstein looked at the clock on the wall. "Lady, it's the middle of the night. Lieutenant Matheson is probably sawing logs by now. You should be, too . . ."

"Listen to me," she interrupted. "I know who the murderer is. You'd better put me in touch with him right away. I think he may strike again soon."

The police sergeant rolled his eyes. A crank call in the middle of the night was just what he did not need.

"This is no joke," Abigail pleaded. "If you'll put me in touch with the lieutenant, I know he'll want to hear what I have to say."

Bronstein sighed. "Lady, it so happens that Lieutenant Matheson just arrested someone for those murders. I don't think he'd appreciate being awakened for your call. Why don't you just relax and call again tomorrow . . . this morning."

"Because it may be too late!" Exasperated, she hung up the phone, thanking her neighbors. Bleary-eyed, they accompanied her to the front door and waved as she ran down the street toward the nearest bus stop. When she was out of sight, they conversed in Spanish about their crazy neighbor. The woman shrugged, the man laughed, and they turned out the porch light.

It had been years since Abigail had taken a bus. She had no idea whether she could catch one this late at night that would bring her to Brighton. And if one did, she still didn't know where the Silvers lived. She'd just have to try calling them again, once she was in the area. It would be the middle of the night, but hopefully they would answer the phone.

Two transfers and an hour and a half later, Abigail got off the bus at the Twelve Corners main intersection in Brighton, and headed for a nearby phone booth. She dialed the Silvers but the line was still busy. Correctly, she assumed their phone was off the hook.

Abigail felt exhaustion creeping into her bones. She hadn't exerted herself in this manner in years. She'd have to be careful . . . she knew she was not in good health.

She dialed Information and asked for the address of the Silvers, but the operator would not give that information, asking her to check her phone book.

"If I had a phone book here, I wouldn't have called you in the first place."

"I'm sorry, ma'am. I'm only allowed to give you the phone number. Have a nice evening."

She hung up, tried another information operator, got the

same spiel, tried it a third time, and was still denied her request.

Close to tears, she hung up the telephone. "Paul, wake up!" she thought. "It's Abigail. Please wake up!"

Johnny Richardson couldn't believe his eyes. Directly across the street from him, making a phone call, was old Witch Hazel. He didn't know or care what she was doing in Brighton, he was just thrilled that he had decided to take a walk when the summer's heat had made sleep impossible for him that night.

He'd never forgotten how Hazel had humiliated him, referring to him as a Dark Child and kicking him out of her house. Her rebuff had stung him mightily, and he'd often thought of trying to get back at her. But she lived so far from him that he'd never followed through on the idea. Now here she was, delivering herself to him on a silver platter!

As he crossed the street toward her, he wished he still had his switchblade. But he could still scare the shit out of her.

Abigail perked up as she saw a young man approaching her. Maybe he even knew the Silvers, or at least be able to guide her to another phone booth where she could look up their address.

As she was about to speak, she recognized Johnny. She felt her heartbeat quicken, hammering out an arrhythmic staccato that made her dizzy.

"Johnny, you must help me."

The boy's laugh sent shivers up her spine. "I'm a Dark Child, Hazel. Remember?"

She gulped the hot night air into her lungs. Breathing was difficult. "Paul . . . Paul is in danger. The Filippo murderer is . . ."

Johnny grabbed her roughly by her shoulders, screaming, "What do you know about the murders?"

"I know who killed them, and I know Paul is in danger of his life. Please guide me to his home." She pressed a hand over her heart; it was throbbing painfully.

"You don't look so good, Abigail," Johnny sneered. "Maybe you'd better sit down and catch your breath."

"No time," she wheezed. But he was right. Was this how a heart attack felt?

Before he did it, Johnny had no idea he would truly harm Abigail. He obeyed the voice inside his head, shouting, "I said, sit down!" As he yelled, he pushed against her with both hands, and watched as Abigail lost her balance and fell hard against a concrete bus bench. Something cracked and Johnny realized what he'd done. He turned to see if anyone was in sight as Hazel moaned in pain on the sidewalk. Johnny looked down to see a small trickle of blood dripping from her forehead to the pavement.

"Jesus," Johnny whispered, and virtually flew across the street to get away from Abigail Alio, sprawled across the ground.

Abigail's last conscious thoughts were an appeal to Paul to awaken, to rescue her and himself. But the pain was too great, and she succumbed to sweet dark sleep.

In his home, safe under a sweat-soaked bedsheet, Paul awoke screaming. As he came fully awake, he shook his head, trying to clear the cobwebs. He couldn't recall what he had been dreaming that had scared him into wakefulness, but he still had the most uncomfortable feeling that something was wrong.

Was there a burglar in the house? Had he heard the noise of someone breaking in? He lay very still, listening for any unusual sounds, but there were none.

He couldn't shake the overwhelming feeling of dread that held him in a hammerlock. The fear would not allow him to get out of bed to investigate. What the hell was wrong?

It took him hours to fall back to sleep.

When a Brighton squad car discovered Abigail Alio at 3:30 A.M. she was already in a coma.

Chapter Twenty-three

Paul was still asleep when his father knocked on his door the next morning.

"Get up, our appointment's in an hour."

Paul grunted, pulled the pillow over his head, feeling dreadful. There was enormous pressure on his head, like he was hundreds of feet underwater. If this headache didn't go away, he'd be in no shape to attempt to make contact with the specter of Mr. or Mrs. Filippo.

Paul got up, walking on shaky feet to his bathroom, where he splashed cold water on his face. He still felt terrible as he walked back to his bed and crawled back under the covers. If he could just get another fifteen minutes of sleep . . .

The second he closed his eyes, he felt himself going under. Shocked but not wanting to let the moment escape, he allowed himself to imagine the mental screen before his tightly shut eyes, watching as it underwent the color change that ended in the brilliant white blank screen. In a moment, the white screen softened, and Paul could already make out the image of someone approaching him through that white mist.

"Who is she?" Lieutenant Matheson asked as he pointed into the darkened hospital room where Abigail Alio lay, her still, frail body connected to a dozen different life support devices.

James Crawford, one of the police officers who'd found

her bleeding on the pavement in the middle of the night, shrugged his tired shoulders. All he wanted was to go home and hit the sack. Stifling a yawn, he answered, "No I.D. on her. We're checking fingerprints now."

Matheson approached Abigail's bedside and stared into the woman's withered features.

"Never saw her before in my life, and I've lived in Brighton for thirty-five years. How'd she get here?" Not expecting a response, he leaned closer to the bed. "She's twitching."

Officer Crawford, caught in midyawn, managed to say, "Beg pardon?"

"I said she's twitching. That mean anything in a coma victim?"

"I wouldn't know, sir."

"Well then, get someone in here who does."

"Yes, sir." Damn. Crawford saw his dreams of going home dissipating as he ran down the hall looking for someone who looked like a doctor.

Abigail watched the entire scene from five feet above her pale bedridden body, and smiled. She knew she was having a near-death experience, but was not frightened. After all, she already knew that death itself was not an end but a blessed beginning, a gateway to life eternal. She welcomed the journey, but was not yet ready to start it. She had one more task to perform.

She focused her mind on Paul Silver, and could feel the boy's confusion and discomfort, but was unable to contact him telepathically—she'd never had the time to teach him what she knew of that form of communication.

Never mind. She could still aid him, by adding her psychic energies to his, helping him contact one of the Filippos and learn their killer's identity.

Dr. Michael Sanders searched through his kitchen drawers for a suitably sharp knife. When he found the serrated steak knife, he smiled and drew it out of its protective sheath.

He allowed the sharp tip of the blade to lightly puncture

a shoulder. With his other hand, he grabbed for the anti-
septic he'd brought with him.

Shivering with pain, Sanders administered to his self-
inflicted wound. Later, he thought, he'd have to get rid of
the bloodied bandage, so that it would appear that he, too,
had been wounded.

The murder method and subsequent alibi had come to
him last night, as he'd sucked on his pipe in his oaken
study. The Silvers, he would claim, had come for a session with him, and an intruder had interrupted their meeting. A fight ensued, and, alas, the Silvers were all killed
by the thief, who had run off with their money after
wounding Sanders.

Now, as he cleaned the blood off his murder weapon,
something very strange happened: In crystal clarity, Sanders realized that he was a very sick person. The realization
struck him like a sledgehammer. What had possessed him
to hurt himself? And worse, to hurt others? Before he
could begin to examine the question clinically, his mind
clouded over.

He was back in control. And more than ever ready to
punish the Silvers—all of them.

"Paul, please! We're running late!"

The sound of his father banging on his locked bedroom
door brought Paul out of his trance. Bone-white from what
he'd learned in his trance state from the specter of Carlo
Filippo, Paul shakily unlocked the door.

When Paul saw his father, tears came in an involuntary
rush. Louis, confused and even a bit embarrassed, cradled
his son's head in the crook of his arm and led him back to
the boy's bed, where the two sat down.

"What is it? You can tell me."

Paul shook his head. "You'll never believe me—never."

"Paul, please."

"It's Sanders. He . . . he's the Brighton axe murderer—
the man who killed the Filippos."

"Jesus Christ, Paul, what in hell are you talking about?
Sanders is a doctor, for God's sake. Why would he . . ."
Then his father went completely silent, and Paul could

read his mind as if it were an open book. His father would never believe Sanders had killed the Filippos. Instead, Paul knew his father would assume it was a drastic way to avoid seeing the psychiatrist again.

"You do not give orders in this house, young man. You do what we think is best for you. And—now, more than ever—I definitely think we need to see Dr. Sanders."

As soon as his father left the room, Paul picked up the telephone. He dialed 0 and asked the operator to put him in touch with the Brighton police. While he waited, he struggled to think of the name of the police officer who'd interviewed him when the Pritchard boy had been killed. Matheson! That was it.

"Brighton police department."

"Uh . . . Lieutenant Matheson, please."

"He's not here.

Paul's eyes bulged. "Then you have to find him. Tell him that Paul Silver knows who the murderer is . . . and tell him I'm afraid he's gonna kill me."

"Is this some sort of prank call?"

Frustrated, yet understanding how strange he must sound to whomever was on the other end of the line, Paul struggled to remain calm.

"Please . . . tell Lieutenant Matheson to come out to Dr. Michael Sanders's office in Pittsford as soon as he can. Please."

"Dr. Michael who?"

"Paul!" His father was coming up the stairs! Paul hung up the phone and ran out to meet him.

"Your father told me, what you said about Dr. Sanders." Virginia exclaimed as they rode toward Sanders's office.

Paul brightened for a moment. Would his mother believe him? "It's true, Mom. Please believe me."

"We'd like to, dear, but we just don't understand . . ."

What could he say? That the specter of Carlo Filippo had come to him and had a conversation with him about the murders? That he'd seen the grisly murders through

Carlo's own eyes? It did sound insane. Paul settled back in his seat and stared vacantly out the window.

Virginia stared at her son silently for a moment, then reached out a hand, clasped it over his, and squeezed.

Dr. Sanders ushered the Silvers into his office, his face beaming, looking about as much like a murderer as Mr. Rogers. It was hopeless, Paul reflected. He'd kept an eye out for a police car as his parents had approached Sanders's office and then parked their car, but to no avail. Obviously, the Brighton police dispatcher had not believed his story. Of course—why should he? Why should anyone?

As Paul took his seat across the table from Dr. Sanders, he realized that his "gift" was actually a curse. He snapped out of his reverie when he heard Sanders address him.

"Suppose you get things started, Paul."

Couldn't his parents see how forced Sanders's smile was? Actually, the man appeared to Paul to be in pain, the grin as plastic as the fruit in the arrangement on the end table by the office door. Paul had noticed that Sanders had locked that door behind them.

Paul was certain that Sanders meant to kill them all, and with mounting fear, the boy was coming to believe there was no way to stop him.

Except . . . except maybe by telling the truth.

Paul matched Sanders's smile and said, "Sure, I'll get things started. We're here because I told my dad that you are the Brighton axe murderer. You killed the Filippos, didn't you?"

Louis raised his arms in embarrassed supplication while Virginia moved nervously in her chair.

"He's been acting like this for a while now, Doctor," Louis began.

Paul cut him off. "You took the axe and chopped off both of their heads at once, didn't you? But first you had to watch them make love, didn't you? You waited until they both had . . . orgasms, didn't you?" It was hard, dreadfully difficult to say those words, but Paul forced them out. As he did so, he watched Sanders's expression turn sour.

Did his parents also notice?

Behind his desk, Sanders slipped his hand into the drawer where he'd hidden the knife, and he grabbed it strongly, pulling it out and resting it on his lap.

The boy had pulled the rug out from under him. Sanders could not delay another minute. He had to kill them all now.

"Paul, come here," Sanders asked softly, motioning to the boy with his free hand. "I want to show you something."

Paul shook his head. "I think you should know that I've already called the police. They should be here any minute."

"Paul, please," his mother implored him. "No more lies. Do what the doctor asks."

"You guys don't know, you don't believe me," Paul shouted, jumping out of his chair. He ran to the office door but it was, as he thought, locked.

"He's gonna kill us all! Don't you see? It's in his eyes! Just look at him!"

"Oh my God," Virginia blurted, starting to cry. What had happened to her son?

"Paul, sit down. Now," his father commanded harshly.

"Mr. Silver, please. I can handle this. It's not actually all that unusual for a patient to harbor this kind of delusion about his doctor. Paul has a problem, I'll admit. But I think I can help him."

Sanders remained seated behind his desk so that the knife would remain hidden, and motioned for Paul.

"Please come here, son."

Wildly, Paul looked around the room for a weapon. Behind Sanders was the only thing he could even hope to use. Slowly, he approached the doctor, who eyed him warily.

"Bad boys need to be punished," Sanders whispered. In a moment, he would leap up and slit the boy's throat in one savage twist of his wrist, and then, while his parents were still too stunned to react, he'd do the same to them. They deserved it, after all—they needed to be punished.

Paul grabbed the umbrella by its ivory handle and, as Sanders's face turned to follow Paul's movement, the boy shoved the tip of the umbrella toward the doctor.

Sanders jumped to his feet, the knife now plainly visible. He grabbed the umbrella away from Paul.

Virginia screamed.

Louis jumped out of his seat and grabbed for the knife. Sanders slashed Silver's extended arm and Louis dropped to his knees, hissing in pain.

"You should have kept your mouth shut, Paul," Sanders shouted. "You shouldn't have told them about me. You're a bad boy, Paul. You need to be punished."

The doctor raised his beloved umbrella and brought it down sharply, smacking Paul across the side of the head. The boy staggered backward, landing in a heap by the office door.

Gunfire erupted behind Paul's dazed head and the door flew open, barely missing Paul's still form. Lieutenant Matheson ran into the room.

"Hold it right there!" he shouted, Magnum pointed directly at Sanders.

With an animallike growl, Sanders launched himself at the police officer, knife aimed at the man's chest. Lieutenant Matheson shot Sanders point-blank in the center of the forehead. The doctor dropped to his knees, his face registering great surprise. He raised a hand to his forehead in disbelief, then flopped onto the floor, inches from Paul.

"Yyyyooouuu . . ." Sanders wheezed, finger reaching toward Paul's body. The bloody digit touched Paul's leg just as Sanders died.

Paul saw Sanders rise out of his body, but another vision overtook this one. Also floating up from Sanders's body was a grotesque caricature of a human being, its body covered with puss-oozing sores, its face the almost unrecognizable visage of a person caught in a fatal fire. It was the most frightening sight Paul had seen, and it was approaching him, reaching out for him, a grotesque parody of a smile stretching across its face.

"You're mine now," Paul heard it croak as it reached closer and closer. Paul was frozen in horror.

Virginia brushed off Sanders's hand like an offensive bug.

"Are you okay, Paul?"

The boy nodded slowly, still dazed from the blow. "Do you believe me now?" he whispered.

"Dear God, yes," Virginia said.

His father joined them. "Forgive us—please?"

Paul hugged them both.

At about that time, in an intensive care ward at a Brighton hospital, Abigail Alio died. Nurses found her body, still warm, a smile on her face.

And somewhere in Hell, a demon shrieked in frustration.

Chapter Twenty-four

"Let me get this straight," Lieutenant Matheson said, staring across his desk at Paul Silver. The boy sat between his mother and his bandaged father. "You're trying to tell me you're . . . what's the word . . . clairvoyant?"

"I don't really know what you call it. I made contact with Mr. Filippo, and he showed me what happened and who killed him."

Virginia interrupted. "Paul's been trying to tell us that he has this power for some time now, but we thought that he was making it up. That's why he was seeing Dr. Sanders."

"Hey, I know how this must sound to you," Louis chimed in. "But the proof is on Paul's side. I mean, you heard enough and certainly saw that Sanders intended to kill us all."

The big lieutenant scratched his head. "Oh, I'm not denying that Sanders was the killer. It's just that this isn't going to look good on my report, not good at all."

He thought about it for a moment. "But if that's your story, that's your story." Matheson looked at Paul, then at the boy's father. "Gonna be pretty tough on you once this story gets out. Media's gonna have a field day with you, son."

The big man looked Paul straight in the eyes. "Are you ready to become a national freak show, kid?"

The ride home from the police department was quiet, everyone's mood somber or reflective as the gravity of their experience hit home. Matheson's remarks were just the icing on the cake.

"Do they have to print a story about me, Dad?"

Louis shrugged his shoulders. "Free press, Sparky. It's bound to come out."

"What are we going to do?" Virginia asked.

"Well, I've been thinking about that. I think the best bet is to be unavailable to the press so that they can't do more than restate the facts in the police report."

"I hope you're right," Virginia whispered.

"I've got another idea, too," Louis said with a smile. "I think it's summer vacation time. And it's gonna be real hard for reporters to track us down at Cape Cod, now isn't it?"

"Yeah!" Paul shouted, surprised at his own enthusiasm. Only then did he realize the tremendous strain he had been under, and the idea of getting away from Brighton sounded like just what he needed.

Virginia's eyebrows raised. "It'll be expensive . . ."

Paul interrupted. "When can we go?"

Louis laughed. "Let's start packing when we get home. Hell, I'll put the vacation on a charge card and we'll worry about it later."

"Outrageous!" Paul yelled.

Virginia smiled warmly. It was a good plan. God knows they all needed the break. And with luck, it would help to keep them out of the public eye—at least until they figured out how to deal with their son's "gift."

By the time they reached their home, Paul was already feeling strangely detached, as if a part of him was being pulled away from the world around him and toward a psychic plane.

Puzzled by his feelings, he excused himself and went to his bedroom. By the time he flopped on his bed, Paul was already watching the screen in his mind's eye turn white, then milky, then foggy. In moments, a figure was approaching him through the mist.

Abigail!

Paul couldn't keep the tears from his eyes. How could she appear to him in a vision unless . . . unless she were dead?

"Why? How?" The questions poured from him between the tears. Paul shivered as he felt Abigail's spiritual essence surrounding him in an embrace, and he was immediately calmed. He wiped tears from his eyes.

"Do not be sad for me, Paul. I was ready for my journey."

"But how . . . when . . . ?"

"The Dark Child," she whispered.

"Johnny! What do you mean? He didn't . . ." He couldn't say it, couldn't even imagine that Johnny could have killed her.

"The boy has fallen prey to the devil."

The devil, Paul thought. Just like Sanders?

Paul's fists were clenched so hard he felt they would pierce his skin at any moment. "I'll kill him. I'll . . ."

Abigail smiled and Paul felt incredible warmth envelop him. "The Dark Child will pay the price in time. Karma is real, Paul. You must remain untainted, for your most important mission still lies ahead."

Paul shook his head. "I don't understand."

"You will—let your nightmares be your guide."

A chill ran up Paul's spine. "No," he protested. "I don't want to be a freak, I want to be normal again."

"Not just yet," she whispered, already just a shimmering shadow.

"Don't go."

"I'll . . . be with you." He could barely hear her now. "And I'll help."

She was gone, and before he knew it, Paul had fallen asleep. He had his drowning dream again, awakening in a cold sweat. Was this the nightmare Abigail had mentioned? He wanted to speak with her again, to ask her what he should do next, to query her about life after death. There were so many questions . . .

But when he tried to concentrate and form the screen in his mind, he found he could not. He was just too exhausted. He fell back to sleep and didn't reawaken for the rest of the day.

Part Two

THE CURSE

Chapter Twenty-five

As Louis Silver loaded the car with his family's vacation luggage, he picked up the rolled-up newspaper on his driveway.

Frowning at the paper, Louis debated as to whether he should open it and search out the inevitable story on the Sanders death. Finally, he pulled off the string that bound the newspaper and it fell open in his hands.

Not surprisingly, news of Sanders's death was spread across the front page. But before Louis had the chance to read the story, his eye caught a smaller headline at the bottom of the same page: "Abigail Alio Succumbs; Longtime Rochester Resident Reputed To Be Practicing Witch."

Louis read this story first, realizing Paul would want to know the details. According to the paper, Abigail had died of a head wound sustained in a fall in Brighton. What had she been doing here? A chill crawled up Louis's spine as he wondered whether she had been trying to find the Silver's house. It seemed crazy, but who knows?

He folded up the front page and carried the paper to the garbage cans on the side of his house. He stuffed the paper into the nearest one. There'd been enough bad news in his family's life these past twenty-four hours. They all needed a rest. Paul had slept all day yesterday and might have slept through today as well if his father had allowed him.

Well, hopefully Cape Cod would be just what the doctor ordered.

*   *   *

Paul was mostly silent for the first half of the ten-hour drive to the Cape. He was worrying about whether he'd lost his power to reach Abigail, and wondering whether to share the news of his communication with her with his parents. Finally, prodded by his parents' worried expressions and attempts to get him to speak, he decided to confide in them.

"It's about Abigail," he said, and noticed how his father's eyes became as big as saucers. "I . . . saw her again yesterday, but it's not what you think."

For a moment he thought his dad was going to drive right off the turnpike, but he brought the car back under control and glanced worriedly at Paul through the rearview mirror.

"See, Dad, she's dead."

Louis cast a glance at Virginia and said, "We know. I read it in the paper this morning and told your mother."

"Paul, do you mean that you . . . communicated with Abigail after she . . ." Virginia was unable to finish the sentence. The whole concept of Paul's powers was still almost so hard to comprehend.

Paul nodded and rubbed at a tear in his eye. "She said there was an important mission I had to perform."

"Jesus," his father whispered. "What does that mean?"

"I don't know, Dad. I can't reach her anymore. I'm having trouble concentrating . . ."

"I'm not surprised," his mother answered. "We all need a rest."

"And resting," his father said forcefully, "does not include attempts to . . . conjure up a ghost . . . even Abigail's. All right?"

Paul understood, but was haunted by Abigail's final words: "Let your nightmares be your guide."

The family fell back into silence, and after a while, Paul was lulled to sleep by the car's motion. Again, he dreamed of the drowning man. He woke up gasping for air, screaming.

Barefoot, Paul led the way along a sandy path that

wound from the cottages to the Atlantic shoreline a half mile away. Two steps back, his father and mother were arm in arm, everyone enjoying the salty breeze and the sound of the seagulls overhead.

Finally, they reached the grassy sand dunes that overlooked the beach. From their perch they examined the nearly deserted beach below.

"Sure is quiet this time of year," Louis offered. "Guess the summer season is officially over, with Labor Day last week."

"I like it quiet," Paul said. "More room to play!" He ran off down the dune, half sliding, half falling till he hit the beach. He kept running till his feet touched the water's edge.

"How's the water?" he heard his mom yell.

"Great!" He started running along the ocean's foamy edge, not thinking at first, just reveling in the sights and smells and feelings of being alive.

After some time, when his parents were just waving specks on the horizon of his vision, he slowed down. To his right he saw a dense overgrowth of tall bushes. He shuffled toward the greenery and spotted a trail that wove through the gnarled branches and lush leafy undergrowth.

Paul wound his way through the naturally formed trail, which led to a small clearing in the middle of a grove of the thick underbrush.

He sat cross-legged in the center of the deserted clearing, concentrating on the far-off sound of the ocean waves crashing against the shoreline. He allowed the sound to overtake his entire consciousness, and soon found himself weaving back and forth to its natural rhythm.

Eyes closed, he was surprised to see a mental image of colors rushing across a screen. In seconds, he was seeing the white vista that preceded one of his spectral visions.

A form began to swirl into shape in the mists.

"Abigail . . . ?"

But the form was male, not female, and at first Paul did not recognize the face that was now just a few feet away.

"Can you hear me?"

A chill crawled up Paul's spine as he placed the strong

Bostonian accent. It was the drowning man! Only this time, he was much more distinct, much easier to understand.

"Joseph Simmons," the man said.

Paul's mouth fell open. He'd recently seen a TV movie based on the life of Joseph Simmons—Mr. Foster, his history teacher, had made everyone in class watch and write a report on it. Paul recalled that the presidential candidate had drowned . . . off the coast of Cape Cod! So that was why it was so much easier to "reach" Simmons here at the Cape. The specter was earthbound to this area.

"I've been drawn to you . . . waiting for you," Simmons said. "Waiting for you to be able to reach all the way through to me." The words floated in and out of Paul's head as if they were carried to him on the surf.

"Why . . . why me?"

"You're strong . . . stronger than you realize. You can make a difference . . ."

Alarmingly, Paul was having trouble keeping Simmons in focus.

"Not your fault," Simmons responded weakly. "Dead too long. Hard to come through, except in dreams . . ."

"What do you want?"

"I was murdered. You must . . . tell everyone . . ."

"Murdered," Paul whispered. "The movie said you drowned. And my dreams . . ."

The apparition shook his head and cloudlike wisps detached from his hair and floated away. "No. Hastings . . . trouble."

Now Paul was losing Simmons altogether. Already, the man was little more than a vague, grayish shape before him.

"Hastings?"

"Presidential candidate . . ." The voice was harder and harder to catch as the image of Simmons grew dimmer by the second.

"He's in trouble?" Paul asked.

". . . danger . . ." By now, Paul was guessing at what Simmons was trying to say. It was like a voice sometimes heard in the background of a long-distance phone call.

Paul couldn't even see Simmons any longer. The man

had obviously used up any remaining spectral strength to reach Paul directly.

Tears came to Paul's eyes. "I don't understand," he cried, looking into the mist. But he could not discern any shape or even a trace of Simmons's aura. All Paul heard were bees buzzing in the bushes around him. All he could smell was the salty ocean air.

And Simmons was gone . . . perhaps forever.

Chapter Twenty-six

Louis took off his glasses and rubbed furiously at his eyes, as if someone had poured salt in them.

Paul wrung his hands. "Don't you see, Dad? Abigail said I had a mission to perform." He stopped. Would they understand?

"Simmons told you that Senator Hasting's life is in danger?" his father said. It was all so incredible. Simmons had been a childhood idol of Silver's. The excellent journalistic skills, the swift political climb.

"Dad," Paul interrupted his father's confused thoughts. "I'm not sure. But he mentioned a killer, and I think he might mean that the same guy who killed him is after Hastings."

His mother slowly nodded, struggling to accept what was happening to her son—to her family. Finally, she said, "So what do we do? If we warn Senator Hastings that his life is in danger, he'll want to know how we know. And let's face it, he'll never believe us . . ."

Louis took hold of one of her hands. "We don't have to do anything at all, you know," he said. "The Secret Service can watch after Senator Hastings. I mean, isn't that what they're paid for?"

Virginia looked dejectedly at the lobster tail on the plate before her. It looked great but she'd lost her appetite. "I don't know what to say. I mean, it's all too much. I thought Simmons drowned. All the papers said he drowned."

"But they never found his body," Louis reminded him. "They were forced to assume he'd drowned."

"Well, why did his . . . killers wait twenty years to strike again? Why do they want to kill Hastings?"

Louis pushed a scallop around his plate, sopping up garlic butter sauce. "Wasn't Hastings Simmon's opposing candidate in that election?"

Virginia searched her memory and shrugged. It was like clearing cobwebs from the corner of a never-used attic.

"You're right, Dad," Paul chimed in. "I remember from the TV movie."

"I wish I'd watched that movie," Louis said, smiling. He sat silently, organizing his thoughts. Finally, he said, "Maybe Hastings found out that Simmons was murdered, and maybe he's going to try to blow the whole thing wide open. After all, it's election year. This would be a bombshell. And maybe certain people can't afford to have their names dragged into a mess like this. I mean, like the Pentagon or the CIA."

"Louis, this isn't a Robert Ludlum thriller. This is real life." Virginia poked the lobster meat and felt bile rising in her throat. She'd definitely lost her appetite. "Lou— what should we do?"

Louis shrugged and glanced at Paul. "What do you think we should do, Sparky?"

Paul wouldn't meet his father's gaze. He really didn't know what to do. More than anything else, he wanted to forget he had his powers, to lead a normal life again. But, if he ignored Simmon's wish, would the terrible drowning nightmares continue—perhaps forever? Until one day, in the middle of one, his own heart would burst?

He looked up at his father. "Dad, Mr. Simmons said I have some pretty special powers. He's been trying to reach me for years—that's where those nightmares came from. He's depending on me.

"I think I've gotta help. At least, I've gotta try."

The waiter walked by their table. "Everything all right?"

"We'll take the check, please," Louis said.

The waiter seemed perturbed. "Sir, you've hardly eaten a thing." He looked around the table, eyebrows flaring. "None of you have. Was the food satisfactory?"

Louis smiled. "It was fine. But I guess the vacation's over. We're going home."

Chapter Twenty-seven

"So what do you think?" Louis asked, hardly daring to look Lieutenant Matheson in the eyes.

Across the desk, the burly police lieutenant stared at his pen for a moment, then lifted his eyes to the Silvers.

"I think you've all been out in the sun too long."

"But . . ." Virginia started, but Matheson held up a halting hand.

"Did you see the papers that came out while you were gone?"

Louis frowned. "I don't see what . . ."

"Did you see any mention of your son's so-called 'power' in the Sanders story?"

"No," Louis admitted. "And I meant to ask you about that. Didn't the reporters believe our story?"

"Are you kidding? Hey, I'm up for a promotion this fall. You think I need to ruin my chances by becoming the laughingstock of the community by explaining that the reason we cracked the Brighton axe murders was because a little boy spoke to the murder victim—a year after he died? Give me a break."

Paul's face reddened. "But you said you believed me!"

"I'm not saying I do and I'm not saying I don't. But the more I sat here and thought about it, the more I realized that I didn't need to explain your part in this whole mess to anyone but my bosses. And they're so happy that this thing is off their books that they don't care how I claim I solved it."

Virginia asked, "Are you saying you won't help us?"

Matheson sighed. "Lady, what do you want me to do—pick up my red hotline and call the White House? I'm a police lieutenant in Brighton, New York."

"Well, what about the FBI?" she persisted. "Couldn't you contact them? Tell them the Sanders story and then maybe they'd believe you."

Matheson was growing impatient, the pulse showing in his temples as he said, "Mrs. Silver, I don't know if I believe your story. I'm just glad that maniac Sanders can't hurt anyone anymore. Anything having to do with a presidential candidate in Washington, D.C., is out of my jurisdiction."

"But . . ." she started.

"Way out." He stood up, his belly casting a shadow over his desktop. "Speaking of which, I'll show you the way out. I have a lot of work to do."

"Now what?" Paul asked his parents, as the family drove home. "Can't we just call Senator Hastings ourselves?"

"If we could reach him, he'd never believe us, Sparky," his father answered. "We need the only thing we can't give him: proof that his life is in danger."

Virginia's eyes lit up. "Do you think you could contact Simmons again?"

Paul looked glumly at his hands. "I've already tried. Mom, I don't think he can be reached anymore."

Virginia felt herself shivering in the summer heat as she wondered just where Simmons had gone. She wanted desperately to ask Paul for details about life after death. But for now, there were more immediate concerns.

Suddenly, Paul snapped his fingers. "Abigail! Maybe I can still reach her. She said she'd be there if I needed her."

Louis said, "Well, son, we need her now."

"Abigail," Paul whispered, eyes closed as he leaned back in his father's comfortable reading chair. His parents watched him intently from the couch opposite him in their living room.

"Abigail, can you hear me?" Paul asked. In his mind's eye, the white screen was turning misty.

Virginia saw Paul smile and nudged Louis. "He must see her," she whispered.

Louis diverted his eyes. He didn't like seeing Paul do this. It was like they were all playing some crazy game. None of this could be real—could it? If it were, it would throw out the window the entire system of beliefs Louis had forged following his mother's death.

Louis looked at his son and, for a moment, felt like he was seeing a stranger who was personally threatening his own sanity.

"I am here," Paul heard Abigail say as her form took shape out of the white mist. She was smiling at him, and he felt her by-now familiar aura surrounding his lovingly.

"You know your task," she said.

Paul nodded. "How did you know?"

"I did not know the true nature of the mission you were to perform. I could only see in your aura a great journey and an even greater responsibility."

"Can you help?" the boy asked.

"I will try. But . . . we haven't much time. Soon I must start my own great journey."

"Louis, he's crying," Virginia whispered, her own lip quivering. She wanted to reach out and touch her son, hold him. But she feared interrupting him in his trance state.

Paul opened his tearing eyes and smiled shyly. "Sometimes I'm just an old crybaby."

Louis shook himself out of his morbid thoughts and rushed to his son's side, embracing the boy with all of his strength. Whatever it was Paul was experiencing, Louis knew in that instant that he was going to be there for the boy.

"What is it, Sparky?" he asked. "What did she say?"

"Just that . . . that we have to hurry."

"What's our next step then?" Virginia asked Louis.

Louis stroked his one-day beard growth. "I guess we take our story to the press."

*   *   *

Martin Hamilton ushered the Silvers into his crowded office. He motioned them into worn chairs and took his place behind his desk, where he lit up a particularly foul-smelling cigar. Once the air was hazy, he began talking.

"So let me get this straight. You said on the phone that you had big news for me about Senator Hastings. That his life was in danger. Why'd you call me? Why not call the FBI?"

Louis answered, "We didn't think they'd believe us. They probably get a dozen crank calls a day."

Hamilton nodded and the thin waft of hair that crossed over the otherwise balding crown of his head flopped up and down. "So why should I be any different? I also get a dozen crank calls a day. Of course, most of them are from my ex-wife . . ." He laughed at his own joke and took a puff off his stogie.

Louis looked at the disheveled man before him and realized he'd made a mistake in coming here. This reporter could surely be of no assistance to them. He stood up and motioned for Virginia and Paul to do the same. They stared at him in confusion.

"I'm sorry," he said. "I think we're just wasting each other's time. Maybe we will try the FBI."

Hamilton slammed the lit butt of the cigar into a dirty ashtray. "Mr. Silver, sit down."

Surprised, Louis did so.

"I know why you came to me."

"You do?"

"I wrote the Sanders story for the paper. And I've had some questions about that story ever since I wrote it. I don't think our local police lieutenant was being entirely candid with me when he explained what happened that day. Now, why don't you help me set the record straight— just to break the ice."

Twenty minutes later, Louis Silver finished talking. Hamilton looked like he was about to chomp through his cigar.

"Bullshit," he announced. Louis blinked as if the word had been a carefully aimed spitball.

"That story is the biggest crock I've ever heard. I'm supposed to believe that your son played 'dial-a-spook' to find out who killed the Filippos? And now he's done it again, and gotten Joe Simmons himself on the 'spirit line.' " Hamilton was finding it hard to contain himself. "Simmons tells your spooky son that he was assassinated, and Hastings is about to be."

The stocky reporter spat the end of his cigar into his ashtray. "You shouldn't be talkin' to me. You should be talkin' to Steven Spielberg." Hamilton guffawed.

Louis countered, "I know how you feel. Hey, I'm a psychology teacher. I've studied the human mind for decades and have never before run into a true . . . clairvoyant, if that's even the word."

"We didn't ask for any of this to happen," Virginia emphasized. "Paul least of all."

Hamilton had stopped laughing and was now regarding Paul as if the boy were some bug under a microscope. "Well, he don't look crazy," Hamilton muttered.

Paul returned his stare. "You want proof."

"Damn straight, kid."

Hamilton led the trio past a bullpen of activity and into an empty conference room. He sat himself at one end of an enormously long oak table, placing his booted feet up on the tabletop.

"On with the show or out you go," he said gruffly, lighting another cigar. Louis approached him, grabbed the half-lit stogie, and slammed it against the sole of the reporter's cowboy boot.

"That's it. We don't need this. We can find another reporter who will listen to us. And someday soon, when you read our story in *The New York Times* or the *Washington Post*, and that story wins its reporter the Pulitzer Prize, you're gonna wish you'd taken us a little more seriously."

Hamilton looked Louis Silver straight in the eye. "You really do believe in this, don't you?"

Silver ignored him. "Let's go, Paul, Virginia."

"No, wait." Hamilton blocked Louis's exit. "Okay, maybe I'm being unfair. Fer Chrissake, put yourself in my place. People are playing practical jokes on me all the time. Hell, once my boss paid a guy to come in and tell me he'd been for a ride on a spaceship, just to see whether I'd take the guy seriously enough to write up the story.''

"Did you?" Paul asked innocently.

Hamilton grimaced. "Why do you think I'm still in this backwater town?" The bearded reporter laughed. "It's not just you I don't trust—it's me. I can't afford any more embarrassments. From here I'll be editing copy for those frigging Laundromat want-ad rags.''

Despite himself, Louis half-smiled. Maybe Hamilton wasn't totally inhuman after all. "Okay, so what's next?" he asked.

Hamilton shrugged his shoulders. He reminded Paul of an ape. "Let the kid strut his stuff.''

"What're you doin'?" Hamilton whispered as Paul closed his eyes and concentrated on lowering his heartbeat while he cleared his mind of extraneous thoughts.

"I'll interpret for Paul," Virginia whispered, "so he doesn't lose his concentration. He tells us that first he needs to completely relax. Then he tunes in to the spiritual plane by envisioning a completely white screen in his mind. Soon that screen apparently turns translucent and the . . . specters come through.''

"Terrific," Hamilton said, shaking his head. "How'm I ever gonna put that on paper?" He watched Paul, who was oblivious to their conversation. Hamilton could see the boy's chest rising and falling very slowly, his mouth barely open. The sound of his intake of breath was loud in the soundproofed room.

"So you say he's gonna contact this Witch Hazel character," Hamilton said. "Will I be able to speak with her?''

"Through Paul," Virginia whispered.

"Terrific," Hamilton said.

Paul was scared. He wanted so badly to convince Hamilton to help them that he was having trouble concentrating. Even now, the screen in his mind's eye was a dirty white, refusing to brighten.

He forced himself to slow his breathing even further and start the color progression again. Slowly, the screen turned from black to deep purple, then royal blue.

Without warning, the screen exploded into deep red. Paul could feel sweat dripping down his armpits as he saw bloody blotches moving toward one another, forming one cohesive mass. The form shimmered and changed, slowly taking on the image of a face.

Paul gasped in terror at the sight of Dr. Sanders.

The dead man's mutilated face twisted into a grimacing sneer. He felt Sanders's hands pushing against his temples.

"You've been a very bad boy," Sanders shouted shrilly in his head. "You have to be punished!"

Paul doubled over in pain as he felt Sanders's fingers dig into the sides of his head. The boy screamed in mortal pain.

"What the hell?" Hamilton looked to Virginia for an explanation of the boy's behavior. Paul was rolling around the floor on his back, doing a bizarre dance of pain.

Passersby were huddled against the window facing the conference room, pointing and shouting.

Louis slapped Paul across the face. The boy groaned and fell limp into Virginia's arms.

Wiping sweat from his brow, Martin Hamilton rose to shaky feet. "Was that it?" he yelled at Louis. "The boy has a goddamned epileptic fit and you're trying to tell me he's talking to a ghost."

Louis was speechless. What had gone wrong?

"Doesn't anyone care about Paul?" Virginia screamed.

Paul's eyelids fluttered open. Slowly, he sat up, hands on either side of his head protectively. He rubbed at his temples.

"What happened, Sparky?" Louis asked, on his knees at his son's side.

"It was . . . Dr. Sanders," Paul said, his voice tinged with fear.

Chapter Twenty-eight

The rat lay on its side by a gutter. Its belly rose and fell slowly as tiny streams of blood flowed from bite wounds along its side.

"Looks like a cat got him," Arnie Brenner guessed as he poked the creature with a long stick.

"He ain't dead yet," Mike Garris observed, hanging back a bit as if he expected the rat to jump up and bite off his nose.

The group of boys started to walk on until Vic snapped his fingers. Like a well-rehearsed drill team, everyone halted and gave their attention to their leader, Vic.

"Listen up," Vic growled, his voice just above a whisper. "As you know, the shit's coming down hard on the Avengers. Ever since the night Johnny Richardson's father called the cops on us, I know it's been tough on some of you guys."

No one said a word, but all eyes turned to Arnie Brenner. He sported a cast on his broken left arm, the result of his livid father's disciplinary action when he'd heard that his son had been caught with drugs that night. Brenner shrugged and smiled.

Gary Gimple offered, "My dad said if he ever heard I was hanging around with you guys that he'd send me to the marines."

The group laughed nervously.

Vic nodded. "Sanders was going to send me to military school." His laugh was chilling even in the midday heat. "Of course, that was before his own plans changed."

As an afterthought, he added, "Old lady Sanders ain't much better. She never wanted me around in the first place. I wouldn't doubt she sticks me in an orphanage any day now."

Vic walked back to where the dying rat lay. "No one splits up the Avengers and gets away with it," Vic said. He snapped his fingers. "Gary, gimme the cherry bomb."

A skinny kid with a pockmarked face handed over something that looked like a huge jawbreaker encased in paper with a string attached.

Vic lifted one foot and placed it on the rat's stomach. The creature squirmed, opening its jowls and squealing in pain. Vic quickly pushed the firecracker in between those jaws, where it stuck. He stepped back and looked at the rest of his gang.

"I got a name for this rat," Vic announced. "Johnny. Johnny 'Rat' Richardson." The group showed their appreciation with raucous laughter and catcalls. Vic hushed them with a hand movement.

Vic retrieved a pack of matches from his pants pocket. "Now Johnny knew when he joined the Avengers that the last thing you do is fuck with us. And ole Johnny here really put the screws to us. Right?"

The other boys nodded and agreed.

Vic bent down and struck a match against the fuse, which lit with a hiss. The rat struggled to close its mouth, but its fangs had clamped into the firecracker.

"Well, ole Johnny is gonna have to learn the hard way that you do not fuck with the Avengers. Right?" Vic took several steps backward and the others quickly followed suit.

The firecracker went off with a hollow bang.

Something slimy splattered against Garris's glasses. With a yelp, he batted the glasses off his face. They hit the hard pavement with a cracking sound.

Vic laughed. "We've got a date with Johnny—at the county fair."

"That's it, then," Louis Silver said, addressing his son. "No more attempts to communicate with the . . . spirit world, or whatever. It's just too dangerous."

"But, Dad, what about Senator Hastings? How will we convince him?"

"Let me worry about that."

"But, Abigail . . ."

His father interrupted him. "Abigail wasn't there to stop Sanders from hurting you. Maybe she needs to be summoned, or maybe she's already . . . started her journey. I don't know."

Paul nodded. His father was right. It hurt just thinking about Sanders's psychic attack yesterday. He didn't know whether he could live through another.

How ironic, Paul thought. Just when he had started to come to grips with his power, he was going to have to shut it off and be a normal kid again. He knew he should feel relief, but somehow he did not.

Maybe it was because of how much he knew he'd miss Abigail. She'd said that Johnny was responsible for her death. And yet he was still alive and free. It was so unfair.

Cheryl Richardson answered the door, smiling when she saw Paul. "We've missed you," she said.

Paul couldn't look Mrs. Richardson in the eyes; it might lessen his resolve.

"Hi, Mrs. Richardson. Is Johnny home?"

"I believe so. Why don't you go up and see for yourself?"

As he strode toward the staircase, he spotted Mr. Richardson in the kitchen, whistling some tuneless melody as he washed dishes. He saw Paul out of the corner of one eye and turned to greet him.

"How you doin', Paul?"

"Fine, sir." He watched as Robert Richardson dried his hands on a towel and approached him. Shoot, now he'd have to be polite.

"And how are you, sir?"

Richardson laughed. "Well, better now, thanks. Life in a jail cell has a way of becoming rather depressing, you know?"

"No, sir."

Richardson laughed more loudly. It seemed to Paul that the man was probably a little drunk.

"No, I guess you wouldn't. And I guess you wouldn't know anything about how I got in jail, either, would you?"

Paul shook his head, feeling more uncomfortable by the moment.

"No, I wouldn't think so," Richardson muttered.

"Honey, please," Cheryl interrupted. "He's here to see Johnny." She placed a hand on her husband's shoulder. Robert brushed it off coldly.

"Here to see my adorable son?" Robert continued. "My loving, respectful offspring?"

Paul watched as Johnny's father staggered over to the refrigerator and retrieved a beer can from its depths. The man popped the top and took a healthy swig.

"Tell that little pig I know what he did," Richardson snarled.

Cheryl gasped. Embarrassedly, Paul backed out of the kitchen, feeling less and less like confronting Johnny. It was obvious this family was already in enough pain.

As he reached the front door, he changed his mind again and ran upstairs. From behind Johnny's closed door came the sounds of the Rolling Stones singing "Sympathy for the Devil."

Johnny leafed through the scrapbook of articles about the Sanders murders. He still couldn't believe that Sanders had been the killer, nor that he'd been killed while attacking the Silvers.

Worse, Johnny was pissed off. Because when Sanders was revealed as the Filippo murderer, Johnny was cheated out of his revenge against his father. And the capper was that, although his father had never mentioned the letter Johnny had written to the police department, the boy knew his father was onto him. Richardson had been treating him like scum ever since he got out of jail.

It was all Paul's fault, Johnny figured. And that's why he felt so good that Witch Hazel had never recovered from her coma. That must really be hurting old Paul about now, Johnny figured.

And then Paul walked into his bedroom.

Eyes bulging, Johnny snapped shut the cover of his scrapbook and tossed it under his bed. "What are you doing here?" he asked moodily.

"We've gotta talk."

"We don't have anything to talk about. Except how you fucked up my life."

Paul was trying hard to maintain control. "Johnny, I know what happened with you and Abigail." He waited for Johnny's reaction.

"What are you talking about?" The words came out at half-volume.

"I spoke with her, Johnny."

"Witch Hazel is dead."

"I spoke with her after she died, Johnny. I know you killed her."

Johnny was about to speak in his defense. After all, he hadn't actually killed her. He'd shoved her, her ankle had twisted, and she'd banged her head against the concrete bus stop. Johnny looked at Paul angrily.

"Get out of here. Get out right now if you know what's good for you."

Paul shook his head. "It won't work, Johnny. You can't scare me." He approached Johnny, pushing against the boy's chest with his forefingers. Caught off balance, Johnny fell backward onto his bed.

"Now you listen to me," Paul said. "You're sick and you need help. I'm going to give you twenty-four hours to call Lieutenant Matheson of the Brighton Police Department. Then I call him."

"And say what? That you talked to a witch after she croaked? He'll never believe you," Johnny said with a sneer.

"I think he will. He knows all about me, Johnny."

The boy's expression turned sour. He felt like he was about to completely break down.

"Twenty-four hours, Johnny," Paul reminded him as he left the room. "Do it for your own sake."

Chapter Twenty-nine

Paul tugged on his father's sweatshirt. "C'mon, Dad, let's go. We'll miss the fireworks."

Louis Silver smiled down at his son. "Relax, Sparky. The fireworks don't start for at least two hours yet. We'll have plenty of time to get to the fair and even ride the double Ferris wheel."

Paul made a funny face and his father laughed. "Dad, you know I'm kinda afraid of heights," Paul admitted.

"Paul, the only way to conquer fear is to face it."

Paul nodded. His dad was right, and the comment applied not only to a county fair amusement attraction, but to his "powers" as well. If the only way to help save Senator Hastings's life was to face the specter of Dr. Sanders, then that's what he'd have to do.

But not tonight, Paul smiled to himself. Tonight was for fun.

"Shitty way to spend a Friday night," Martin Hamilton complained aloud to his cat, which looked up from a half-eaten dinner of noxious-smelling "cat tuna."

"Waste of my time and talents," Hamilton continued as he reached into his hall closet for a lightweight jacket. "Covering county fairs and beauty contests for some backwater rag when I should be covering the elections for *Time* magazine."

At one time, Hamilton had come close to that goal. In his early thirties, he'd worked his way up the ranks at the

L.A. *Times* to star status as a political reporter. But he'd developed a drinking habit that had gotten him in trouble one time too many, and finally he'd been fired. Unable to find other newspaper work on the West Coast, he'd returned to his hometown, Rochester, where he'd joined the staff of the local daily. But his reputation had preceded him, and instead of being the head of a department, he'd been given only a reporter's title, covering the stories the other reporters had turned down.

He'd fought for the shot at covering the Filippo murders as a chance to prove to his bosses that his copy still sold papers. They were impressed with his coverage of both the murders and the Sanders wrap-up story, but were still sending him out on these feature bits more often than not.

Hamilton was tired of paying his dues. And that's why he'd initially agreed to see the Silvers yesterday. He was working the news desk when Louis Silver had called in, and his story sounded intriguing enough to follow up. But after seeing the Silver boy's demonstration of his "powers," Hamilton had been upset and put off. What did they take him for—a nut case?

Still, Hamilton admitted as he locked up the house and headed for his car, Silver's mention of the Pulitzer Prize had been haunting him ever since he'd booted the angry parents and their weird kid out of his office.

Had he judged the situation too quickly? Or even incorrectly? Normally, he trusted his reportorial instincts. In this case, though, maybe—just maybe—the Silvers were worth one more meeting. He'd think about it tonight, while he was walking the midway at the Brighton County Fair.

"The county fair? You can't go," Robert Richardson said. "You're grounded."

"For how long?" Johnny Richardson asked angrily.

"Until you admit that you wrote the letter that put me in jail."

Johnny grimaced. Well, fuck him, he thought. As soon as his father and mother were glued in front of the TV set for the evening, he'd sneak out the upstairs window, crawl down the latticework on the side of the house, and head to the fair anyway.

After all, he thought as he retreated to his bedroom, he had an appointment to keep—with Paul Silver.

Johnny reached under his bed and retrieved a kitchen knife. If he cut up Paul a little, just enough to fuck up his face or something, maybe he could regain his place with Vic, and the Avengers.

"Avengers, assemble!" Vic Filippo shouted. Half a dozen boys stopped talking and gathered in a circle around their leader.

Filippo looked beyond them to the colored lights of the fair's midway.

"It's real crowded down there," he said softly. The circle of boys tightened around Vic to better hear his words. "Lots of fish out there tonight. Lots of wallets hanging out of pockets, purses waiting to be grabbed. Soon as the fireworks start and everyone's attention is on the sky show, that's when you get started."

He looked at his watch. "We meet back here at eleven. If you've got less than a hundred dollars on you, don't bother coming back at all. Got it?"

The group nodded.

"One more thing," Filippo growled. "Johnny Richardson. If you see him, I want him. Alive." He laughed and added, "For the moment."

Chapter Thirty

Wet straw and spun sugar were the smells of the Brighton County Fair on that cool summer's night.

The sounds were myriad and difficult to distinguish: cars gunning their engines or screeching to a halt, music blaring from tinny speakers. Scores of teenagers, yelling greetings to friends they'd not seen since the end of the school year. Amateur and professional barkers, enticing patrons to booths and rides. Screams and laughter from those braving the rusted, rickety rides.

The sights: enough colored lights to blot out the stars in the clear black sky overhead. Neon lights that buzzed like angry hornets, bulbs blinking in a thousand different patterns.

Faces, young and old, handsome and pretty, plain and ugly, features sharpened by the lights' unflattering glare. Smiling faces, stuffing oversized candied apples or mustard-dripping hot dogs between their teeth.

People everywhere: in lines for the concession stands, rides, and games. Paul and his parents were in line for the double Ferris wheel. Paul hopped from one foot to the other nervously, a dancer on a sizzling griddle. He really didn't like heights.

They reached the front of the line, and already his parents were being ushered into the metallic chair. He squeezed next to them and a restrictive bar was being shoved against his stomach.

The Ferris wheel began its ascent with a jerk that sent

their car swinging back and forth precariously. Louis laughed while Paul gripped the metal bar with all his might.

The ride came to life with a squeal of metal against metal. Somewhere a record started, coming slowly up to speed: Mitch Ryder and the Detroit Wheels singing, "Jenny Take A Ride."

Paul saw his parents sneaking a kiss. Embarrassed, he turned his attention to the crowded midway on display beneath him. He watched the people gain and lose their features as the Ferris wheel spun close to ground and then back into the sky. Was that Anne Basehart, the pretty cheerleader he had a crush on, walking toward the hot dog stand? In the next moment she was lost in the crowd as the wheel turned upward.

As the Ferris wheel approached the ground again, Paul felt his stomach rise to his throat as he spotted Johnny Richardson heading toward him. When the wheel rose again, he watched as Johnny weaved through the crowds past the Ferris wheel. At the wheel's apex, Paul's heart flipflopped again as he saw Vic Filippo trailing a few yards behind Johnny.

By the time the double Ferris wheel had slowed to a stop, the two were swallowed up by the crowd. It was as if they had disappeared . . . or had never been there in the first place.

Chapter Thirty-one

Vic Filippo sneered. He couldn't believe his luck. He'd been looking for some fat wallet to pinch when he'd spotted Johnny Richardson not more than ten feet away. Vic had immediately dropped back to make sure that he was invisible in the mass of people strolling the midway.

Vic had been following Johnny for ten minutes now, hoping to link up with one of his fellow Avengers. He didn't particularly want to face off with Johnny without at least one witness, but in the end he'd decided it didn't really matter who saw the Avenger take his revenge.

Now he could barely suppress his laughter when he saw Johnny join the line of people waiting to enter the walk-through funhouse. Vic got in line, making certain he was far enough back so that Johnny wouldn't spot him until it was too late.

It was too bad things had come down as they had, Vic reflected. Johnny was an okay kid, but that no longer mattered. Ever since the night that Johnny's dad had busted up their party, Vic knew it was his responsibility to set things right again. After all, he was the one who had sponsored Johnny's membership in the Avengers. Too bad it was to be so short-lived.

Johnny was pissed. He'd snuck out of his house with no problem, and had been wandering the fair for over an hour now with no sign of Paul Silver. If he didn't get back home soon, his parents were sure to discover he was not in his

167

bedroom. They always came upstairs to bed right after
Dallas.

He'd already decided to head home when he passed by
the giant clown's face whose mouth was the entrance to
the House of Fun. Johnny'd decided not to let the evening
be a complete waste—he'd always liked fun houses. Besides, the line was pretty short. Most people were beginning to make their way to the field where the fireworks
were about to begin.

Martin Hamilton placed his jacket on the grass of the
playing field and sat down heavily. He was thoroughly
bored and tired to boot. As soon as the blasted fireworks
were over, he'd pack it in and write the story tomorrow
morning.

He was still settling in when he spotted the Silver
family, dropping a blanket on the forty-yard line. Hamilton started to yell to them, then stopped. Did he really
want to get reinvolved with this bunch of crazies (but what
if they weren't?)?

"Fuck it," he muttered. At least their company would
keep him from falling asleep during the fireworks display.
He stood up and waved, yelling to them.

Louis Silver spotted the reporter. Of all the places to run
into this guy . . . To his great surprise, Hamilton approached them with hand outstretched. Silver pretended he
didn't notice it.

"How are you, Mr. Silver?"

Virginia Silver bristled. "What do you care, Mr.
Hamilton?"

Hamilton held his hands above his head in mock surren-
der. "You win. I was an asshole. I admit it. My apolo-
gies." He bent down to where Paul was seated. The boy
was attempting to ignore him.

"I don't blame you for not liking me. You put your
trust in me and I blew it. Maybe you'll give me a second
chance?"

Louis answered for him. "That won't be necessary, Mr.
Hamilton. You see, Paul won't be using his power anymore. He was attacked that day in your office, by the

specter of Dr. Sanders. Another attack like that one . . .''
Louis shrugged. "Hell, just forget it. I don't expect you to
believe me and I don't care.''

"Hey, when you get to know me, I'm not really such an
ogre,'' Hamilton said. "Least, I didn't used to be.'' He
looked around him. The field was rapidly filling up.

"Looks like I lost my spot,'' he remarked. "Mind if I sit
here?''

Before anyone could answer, the floodlights covering
the playing field dimmed. Any response from the Silvers
was lost in the lusty cheering of the crowd.

The show was about to begin.

Johnny entered the fun house through the open mouth of
the wall-sized clown face. In the clown's mouth, a giant
barrel revolved, which Johnny negotiated easily. He rounded
a darkened corner and felt the floor give way. He stepped
backward, then renegotiated his step. The wood had been
replaced by pillows. Johnny grinned. This was fun.

Vic ran through the revolving barrel moments later,
making sure he was out of Johnny's sight. He couldn't
allow himself to be seen till the right time.

Most of the light in the funhouse came through cracks
in the makeshift walls. Suddenly, that light blinked out
and Vic was surrounded by total darkness. He nearly
panicked for a moment until he realized that the midway
lights had been turned out for the fireworks display.

Somewhere up ahead, he heard screaming from people
apparently not thrilled about being left in darkness. It was
perfect for Vic, though.

Johnny weaved through a tilted room like a drunkard,
laughing as he tried to adjust his eyes to the sudden
dimming of light. He could barely see the doorway ahead
of him that led up a narrow, creaking staircase. If he
remembered correctly from what he'd seen while in line,
at the top of the stairwell was a series of fun house
mirrors and then a long slide that led to the exit.

*   *   *

His eyes adjusting to the darkness, Vic thought he could make out Johnny's form ahead of him. He took the switchblade out of his pocket and clicked the switch. The blade whooshed open silently.

The first firecracker burst deafeningly above the fun house.

Johnny laughed at his grotesque image in the warped mirror. In its reflection, he saw someone approach him from behind. Johnny blinked against the darkness as he saw something shiny glinting in the afterglow of the fireworks.

A tremendous explosion deafened Johnny and the room went white from the massive pyrotechnic display overhead.

Vic stumbled forward blindly toward where he last saw Johnny. He bumped into the boy and heard him grunt. Vic plunged his knife into pliant flesh.

Another bomb burst overhead and Johnny's face was caught in photographiclike display as it registered agonizing pain from the knife blade. His scream was lost to the sound of the bomb's burst.

Five more rockets hit the sky and exploded, bathing the scene below in a deep red wash.

Johnny fell to his knees gasping, as Vic Filippo stood above him. The room went from deep red to violet to black again as Johnny retrieved his own knife from a backpack.

Johnny lunged upward and felt the knife's blade rip through Vic's pant leg just below his crotch. Vic hissed in surprise and pain, falling to the dusty floor next to Johnny. "You bastard," he groaned through clenched teeth. The two exchanged knife thrusts but their shrieks were lost in the noise of the skyrockets overhead.

Vic twitched involuntarily, his last thought of the many frogs he'd dissected. He must look a lot like them right now . . .

Johnny smiled. His weird fantasy had finally been played out. He'd experienced the thrill of the kill.

Johnny looked down at his own chest, where blood was gushing in an ever-widening pool. His breath was coming in short gasps. He guessed he was dying but it didn't matter. In fact, it was perfect. He knew he was about to experience the biggest thrill of all.

Johnny Richardson took his last breath and expired in the House of Fun.

And somewhere a demon screamed in ecstasy.

"Guess that's it," Virginia said as she stood and stretched.

"No way, Mom. There's still the grand finale," Paul reminded her.

"There they go," Martin Hamilton announced as he heard the muffled crumps of sound as a dozen rockets were fired simultaneously. Everyone held his breath in delicious anticipation.

The sky was suddenly alive with colors as starburst after starburst of light exploded into full bloom directly overhead. The crowd burst into applause and cheers.

Paul Silver screamed and fell back to the grass.

"Sparky—what's wrong?" his father shouted, but inside, he knew.

"What's the problem?" yelled Hamilton.

"It's that bastard, Sanders," Louis screamed as he grabbed his son's shoulders. Paul went limp and opened his eyes, looking into his father's concerned face.

"He's dead, Dad," Paul said.

"Who?"

"Johnny's dead. And Vic Filippo, too."

Chapter Thirty-two

"It's . . . so hard to believe," Martin Hamilton spluttered and shook his head as he watched the ambulances pull away, their sirens wailing like banshees in the night air.

His arm around his son, Louis Silver could feel Paul shivering.

"Maybe now you'll believe us, Mr. Hamilton," Paul said. His voice was a weak whisper against the growing commotion of police in the fun house. Paul had led the authorities directly to the spot where Vic and Johnny's bodies had been found.

"All I know," Hamilton said, "is that I need a cup of coffee."

The Silvers picked a table in the back room at Don and Bob's. Hamilton sipped at some coffee, his hands none too steady against the sides of the cup.

"So you say that you were watching the fireworks and all of a sudden . . ."

Paul finished the sentence for the struggling Hamilton. "All of a sudden, there was Johnny, right in front of me, and I was feeling the pain he was feeling when Vic stabbed him. Then I saw, through Johnny's eyes, as he stabbed Vic and then I saw Vic fall on top of me . . . I mean, Johnny. And then . . ." He couldn't finish the sentence.

"We know, honey," Virginia said softly, taking one of her son's hands in hers and rubbing it.

"Incredible," Hamilton whispered.

Paul looked straight into Hamilton's bloodshot eyes. "You didn't answer my question: Do you believe us now? About Mr. Simmons? And Senator Hastings?"

Hamilton examined the bottom of his empty coffee cup as if reading tea leaves. He slowly nodded.

Paul brightened. "And will you help us?"

The reporter sighed. "I guess I have no choice."

Upstairs, Paul sipped hot chocolate while his father tucked him in.

"Think you can sleep, Sparky?"

The boy shrugged his shoulders. He was exhausted but he was also buzzing like a toy that had been overwound.

Paul said, "Johnny was . . . pretty sick, huh, Dad?"

His father nodded.

"But in the end," Paul said, "when he knew he was dying, he reached out to me. It was like he was trying to ask me to forgive him."

"Do you?"

Paul wiped a tear from his eye. "Yeah. And, Dad—I'm gonna miss him."

The two sat silently for a while. "I think I'm tired enough to sleep for a week," Paul said.

Louis smiled and bent over his son to kiss his forehead. "I love you, Paul," he whispered, as he turned out the boy's reading light and quietly left the room.

When he was certain that his parents thought he was sleeping, Paul turned on his reading lamp and stared at the ceiling. Ever since that horrifying vision of Sanders at the newspaper office, Paul had been afraid of the dark.

And, while he didn't want to worry his dad, he was really too upset about Johnny to fall asleep. He wished he could "turn on" his power right then and there to contact his friend. But he lived in fear of a return visit from Dr. Sanders.

What he needed, Paul decided with a sigh, was Abigail.

She had promised to protect him. But when he'd needed her, when Sanders had psychically beaten him to within an inch of his life, she had failed to appear.

Where was she? Paul wondered. Was she already on that final journey to the next level of existence . . . whatever it was? Paul shivered. So many questions remained to be answered about what lay beyond death's door. And now, with Sanders just waiting to grab Paul's soul, those questions would have to remain unanswered.

Part Three

THE POWER

Chapter Thirty-three

An hour after their plane had touched down at Washington National Airport, Martin Hamilton and the Silvers had checked in at the Marbury House in Georgetown and Hamilton had phoned Hastings's press secretary.

Paul could hardly contain himself. "Did you talk to him? When is he gonna see us?"

Hamilton held up a hand. "Who wound you up?" Stepping inside the Silvers' hotel room, he nodded to Louis and Virginia, who were busily unpacking.

"Well?" asked Virginia.

"Well . . . we'll see," Hamilton said, noting the long faces before him. "I know what I promised, and I intend to deliver. Just let me talk to him first myself, to tell him what I experienced firsthand."

"He'll never believe us," Paul said. "We should've never come here."

Hamilton placed a friendly hand on the boy's shoulder. "Just wait and see."

At nine the next morning, a stretch limo was parked in front of the Marbury House.

"This is . . . incredible" was all Louis Silver could say as he was led to the waiting limo by Martin Hamilton, looking like the cat that had swallowed the canary.

"You must have been very persuasive," Virginia said excitedly, "to get him to agree to meet with us so soon."

"You can say that again," Hamilton laughed as he

ushered the Silvers into the limo, where they received their second surprise of the day: facing them, hand outstretched, was Senator Jarred Hastings himself.

"Welcome to Washington," he said in his famous bellow. Hastings looked even more handsome in person than on TV. The dimpled cheeks, gleaming, clear green eyes, and curly brown hair somehow disguised at least ten of his fifty years.

Louis was the first to shake himself free of his stargazing. "Thanks very much for seeing us."

"I hope you don't mind the secrecy. There are some kooks out there who'd love to know my itinerary. But then, you seem to know that." He winked conspiratorially at Paul, who felt both mortally embarrassed and very important all at once.

"Should we explain . . . ?" Louis started. Hastings shook his head.

"I love this town. Let me show it off to you." Hastings tapped on the window separating the spacious rear section from the driver's compartment. The car began to roll forward, its movement nearly imperceptible inside.

As the car drove through the city, Hastings kept his passengers entertained with stories of his political career. He'd worked his way up the political ladder slowly but surely, starting in local government almost thirty years ago, graduating to mayor, governor, state senator, culminating in his unsuccessful bid for the presidency back in '68.

"The year Joseph Simmons was killed," Paul chimed in.

"Yes, he did tragically pass away that year. And who would have guessed Joe's brother would throw his hat in the ring to take Joe's place. Or that he'd win."

Hastings interrupted his memories to point out the window at the White House, which had just come into view. The driver automatically slowed as he steered past the front lawn of the Presidential mansion. Fountains created a rainbow that glistened radiantly in the noonday heat.

"It's beautiful," Virginia whispered.

"My future home address," Hastings laughed. Louis and Martin exchanged glances.

The driver turned a corner and Paul was the first to point out the white needle pointing to the sky. Like everything else they'd seen that day, the Washington Monument was even more impressive than any photographs could show.

"Can we stop?" Paul asked.

Hastings smiled. "Not right now, son. But you can come back anytime before midnight. Summer hours," he explained. "And the view at night is outstanding. Washington from five hundred fifty-five feet up is . . . well, breathtaking."

The senator glanced at his watch. "Let's get down to business." He rapped on the glass partition. "The Rayburn Building, please."

Chapter Thirty-four

Hastings guided his guests into an office that spoke of his rural roots: quilted covers on soft couches and rocking chairs, farm tools nailed to dark wooden walls, paintings of pastures and grazing cows.

"All of this," Hastings gestured around the room, "just helps to remind me of the real world beyond politics. Keeps me balanced."

Hastings sat down and motioned for Hamilton and the Silvers to do the same.

"Now what's all this about my life being in danger?" he asked Paul.

Paul shifted uncomfortably in his chair. "I hardly know where to start . . ."

"Maybe I can help," the politician offered. "Mr. Hamilton here has already described what happened to you back in upstate New York. I must confess, I've never run into a true . . . psychic before."

"I'm not really psychic, Mr. Hastings, sir. I can't see into the future." Paul felt his face turning beet-red. "I can just . . . well . . . communicate with people who have . . . well, you know, died."

"Well, I think that's quite a talent in and of itself. So you mean that you could conjure up, let's say, Abe Lincoln for me right now?"

Virginia bit her lip to keep from interrupting. She could see how uncomfortable Paul was. But the family had already spoken about how to handle this interview, and it had been agreed that Paul would have to do most of the talking.

"No, sir," Paul responded. "You see, people sort of 'come to me'—I don't really know how to reach them. I'm kind of like a radio, receiving signals from these people. And anyway, I found out that most people, once they're dead, go on to . . . someplace else."

Hastings leaned forward, his elbows on his desktop. "And where's that?"

"I don't really know."

"I should think you'd want to know. I mean, if you knew what happened to people after they died, why, you'd be the biggest celebrity since Christ."

"I doubt that, sir. I mean, just because I know what I'm saying is true, that doesn't mean anyone else would believe me." He paused. "Do you believe me?" Paul asked.

Hastings stared beyond Paul, beyond the walls of his office and into space for a moment before answering.

"I . . . don't know yet, Paul. But I'm willing to listen. Tell me about Joe Simmons. Why didn't he 'go on' to this mysterious 'other place' you mentioned? I mean, he's been dead for two decades."

"Yes, sir, but I guess Mr. Simmons stuck around because he was . . . well, he was mad. See, he says his death was a murder, not an accident."

Hastings's bushy eyebrows raised a quarter inch.

Paul went on. "And Simmons asked me to warn you . . ."

"To warn me?"

"He said there were killers after you. I mean, I think that's what he said. He was a little hard to understand."

Hastings smiled. "Death has a way of doing that to people." Then he turned serious. "Did he tell you who killed him?"

Paul shook his head.

"Then how do I protect myself . . . ?"

"Senator Hastings," Louis interrupted. "I think that's a job for the FBI."

"Of course, you're right, I'm sorry." He wiped the sweat off his brow with a silken handkerchief.

"Time for me to explain why I brought you here,"

Hastings said. "I mean, I've been threatened before. Usually I shrug it off as some disgruntled taxpayer. But when Hamilton explained what had happened to him at that county fair, and then when he mentioned Joe Simmons . . . Well, I knew I had to see you.

"You see, I've been getting these phone calls in the middle of the night at my home. Never long enough to trace. Just someone calling to say, 'We got Simmons and we're gonna get you.' "

Hastings stopped to let the impact of his statement sink in. Virginia's hand went to her mouth. Martin Hamilton was scribbling furiously into a notebook.

"That's not for publication, Mr. Hamilton," Hastings added.

"You . . . don't think we made those calls, do you?" Louis asked.

"Believe me, Mr. Silver, I know you didn't. After Mr. Hamilton left yesterday, I had the FBI do a little check on you." Hastings pulled a manila envelope out of his top desk drawer. "File's right here, if you'd care to see it."

Louis blanched. "The FBI has a file on us?"

Hastings laughed. "Oh, nothing serious. You were a bit radical in college, Mr. Silver. The usual antiwar marches and such. But really, your entire family gets a very clean bill of health."

Hastings could see Silver's expression turning from surprise to anger. "Please," the politician said, setting the file folder back in his desk and shutting the drawer. "Look at it from my point of view. You'd have done the exact same thing, especially after these phone calls."

"Of course, of course," Louis admitted.

"But that's why I wanted to see you. And while I still don't know who is threatening me, at least now I can get the FBI to take those threats more seriously."

Hastings stood up, signifying the end of their interview. He extended a hand to Paul and shook it heartily. "So you see, you've done me a very big favor, young man. I'll always be in your debt."

He turned to Louis and Virginia. "You and your family are true citizens, Mr. Silver. You can be very proud of

yourselves and of Paul.'' He shook their hands and ushered them to the door to his office, where he stopped,
blocking their exit.

"If I were you," Hastings said in little more than a
whisper, "I wouldn't tell anyone else about your Washington visit, or your son's . . . power. There are people in
this city who would pay well to be able to study Paul in
. . . shall we say, a less than pleasant environment."

Louis nodded. "Agreed. And besides, Paul isn't using
his power anymore. I think he'll enjoy being just a normal
kid again, right, Sparky?"

"Yep."

"And you, Martin," the politician concluded. "I also
owe you more than I can ever say. Please know that, when
I win this election, you'll always have access to me. And I
do plan to win, you know. I've been working toward this
goal for my entire political career. There's a lot of work to
be done to clean up the mess this country is in . . . and I'd
like a shot at it."

Hamilton was positively beaming, fastasizing picking up
the phone in Rochester, New York, and dialing a number
that connected him to the President of the United States.
Hell, with that kind of status, he'd be at *Time* or *Newsweek*
overnight. He thanked Hastings profusely and everyone
said farewells. Their limo awaited.

Once he was alone again, Hastings retrieved the folder
marked "Silver" from his desk drawer. He opened it and
stared at the first draft of his presidential inauguration
speech.

Chapter Thirty-five

It was dusk. Through the haze of exhaust fumes, the sun covered the sky in a crimson swath. In view was the Washington Monument, standing in dramatic white relief against the sky. Paul insisted the group stop at the monument for some photos.

The limo drive parked and the few tourists at the site looked their way, hoping to see a Washington celebrity. They turned away disappointedly when they failed to recognize the car's occupants.

With the sun already beyond the horizon, the air had mercifully begun to cool. A soft breeze carried further relief from the day's humidity.

Paul led the way to the monument's entrance.

"Race you to the top, Dad!"

"Where do you get your energy?"

"I'm betting it's a tied race," Martin commented, pointing to an elevator. "That's the only way up or down."

"Well, let's go," Paul prompted them.

Hamilton held back. "Sorry, heights and me don't agree. I'll hang with the limo driver—see what kind of good gossip I can pick up."

Paul was already in the elevator, and his parents soon joined him. The doors whooshed shut and the elevator began its minute-long ascent, a prerecorded tape explaining the history of the monument.

Finally, the doors opened again. A few other late tourists were peering out of the long, narrow windows.

Virginia couldn't find the words to describe her emotions as she glanced out the nearest window at the Washington skyline. Straight ahead, beyond a long, reflective pool, was the Lincoln Memorial. In another direction she could see the outline of the White House. A glance behind her offered the outline of the Capitol Building.

Looking at these structures, so symbolic of America's history as a free country, Virginia felt more strongly than ever that her family had done its patriotic duty warning Hastings.

She turned to Louis, who was similarly mesmerized by his surroundings.

"Do you think he really believed us?" she asked softly.

It took Louis a moment to respond. "I don't know. I just know we've done all we can do."

"Will he make a good president?" she asked.

Louis shrugged. "Compared to what? Name me a president who wasn't a little crazy . . ."

Paul interrupted them. "We're not outside."

"What?" Virginia said.

"I thought we'd be outside. You know, in the open air."

"Too dangerous," Louis answered. "This place would be the suicide capital of the world . . ."

Paul smiled. "I'm kinda glad, actually. You know I don't like high places usually, but this is really great!"

Louis grinned, ruffling his son's hair. "Ready for some dinner?"

He nodded and they turned toward the elevator just in time to see its doors close silently. Virginia groaned.

"Well," Louis said, "looks like you get to race me after all . . . all the way down." He pointed to the stairwell.

Paul brightened. "Yeah!"

A guard stepped out of nowhere, startling all of them.

"Sorry, folks," he said in a southern drawl. "Stairs are closed—have been for years. You'll have to wait for the elevator."

"Yes, sir," Paul said, staring at the man's uniform, which hung as loosely from his body as a bedsheet. The man looked like a circus clown, Paul thought.

He turned to see his parents taking a stroll hand in hand toward the opposite end of the room. Paul smiled as he watched them sneak in some kissing.

In the next instant, Paul was grabbed roughly by the shirt collar, one big hand slapped over his mouth so his screams would not be heard by his parents.

, Paul was astonished to recognize the guard as his captor, as the man jerked Paul into the stairwell and slammed shut the door. Next to the door, slumped against a wall in his underwear, was an unconscious man. Obviously the real guard, Paul thought, his mind a tangle of confusion and fear.

Paul saw the stairwell tilt onto its side as he felt himself being lifted higher and higher, despite his struggles. When would his folks notice he was missing?

The boy tried to scream but the man's hand was blocking his mouth. Paul took a big bite out of the flesh in front of his face, and felt the hand twitch. But the grip remained firm.

Paul felt his stomach turn over as he realized that the man was going to toss him over the guardrail and down the space between the stairs. He closed his eyes.

"Hey!" It was his father! The attacker shoved Louis, who fell back against the concrete wall. He rebounded, hitting the imposter against the knees with all his weight.

Paul felt himself falling and, a moment later, hitting the cold metal stairs. He opened his eyes and saw the assailant fleeing downward.

Louis leaped over the guardrail, barely clearing the dark space between the stairs, and landed roughly against the metal stairwell one level down. He hissed in pain from a twisted ankle but managed to grab the attacker's foot. The man went sailing, landing with a terrible cracking noise against one of the concrete walls. He lay still, panting slowly.

Louis limped back up to Paul, who sat in a daze. "Are you okay, Sparky?" His pain was evident in his tight-throated voice.

The boy nodded, rubbing at an elbow. "Hit my funny bone."

Could have been worse, Louis thought, looking beneath his feet at the space between the stairs. They were still at least two hundred feet from the bottom of the darkened stairwell.

The two helped each other up, and made their wobbly way down to where their assailant lay, still unconscious.

"I wish I'd broken his neck," Louis growled.

They stepped over the man and made their way slowly down the rest of the stairs.

Virginia met them at the ground-level exit, her face a mask of fear. Behind her was a guard, who quickly ran past the group and up the stairwell.

Virginia fell into her husband's arms. "Oh, Lou, what happened?"

"It's okay now, Ginny," Lou said.

Hours later, Louis and Paul had been treated by paramedics and questioned at length by the police. Finally, the group was driven back to their hotel by the exhausted limo driver.

"So who was this guy?" Hamilton asked. "A terrorist?"

"The guy won't identify himself," Louis said, "so the police are running a fingerprint check."

Virginia cupped her son's hands with her own. "I've had enough intrigue," she sighed. "Let's get a good night's sleep and head home."

Paul wished he could sleep. But lately his dreams had been plagued with visions of Abigail crying out to him. What was wrong? he wondered. And how could he help?

Chapter Thirty-six

He could hear his father snoring in the next room, but sleep would not come to Paul Silver. He'd tossed and turned for hours and finally given up. Now he lay in bed, his reading lamp dispelling the room's darkness.

He had to admit it: he was scared stiff. He was certain the attack at the Washington Monument was no coincidence, that somehow Simmons's killers had learned of Paul and were stalking him. Even back home in Rochester, Paul wondered whether he could elude their reach.

And then there was Abigail. Paul had been too frightened to respond to her psychic attempts to reach him. He felt enormous guilt, overshadowed only by a vague fear of something truly evil ahead that he did not want or have the strength to confront.

What was it his dad had said? To conquer fear, he had to face it. Easy for you to say, Dad. You don't have a maniac inside your head, just waiting for the chance to take over your brain . . . or your soul.

He had to stop thinking such thoughts, Paul told himself, or he was going to go nuts. He had to do something.

Trouble was, the boy thought, his dad was right. Paul could go through life a scared wimp, or he could deal with his problems . . . even ones as immense as these.

First things first, then, Paul thought, sitting up in bed and clearing his mind. He had to attempt contact with Abigail Alio . . . wherever she was.

* * *

In the gray, featureless vista that marked the geography of the land between life and death, Abigail Alio was a prisoner.

Since dying, she'd chosen to postpone her own spiritual journey to stay close to Paul. While she hadn't wanted to frighten the boy, she was aware of an evil presence that hovered around Paul like a moth drawn to a flame.

Worse, when Sanders died, his spirit had combined with the malevolent force around Paul, and she had been overpowered.

Now, she could feel Sanders sucking away at her dwindling psychic energies like a ghostly vampire. Soon he would possess her eternal soul, and she would cease to exist on the spiritual plane altogether. It was the ultimate blasphemy—the quintessential horror.

After a seeming eternity of agonizing pain, she felt Sanders's grip on her psychic energies lessening. For the moment, he was satiated. He would leave her alone for a while, as he rested after his "meal." This was his only vulnerable time, but it was also the time when Abigail was at her weakest.

Yet she knew she had to fight him, for her own sake, as well as Paul's.

Then, in a burst of soothing white light, she felt Paul's presence. Was it possible? Had he chosen this moment by coincidence to attempt contact? Or had he somehow felt her waning spiritual energies calling out for help?

"Paul." She was so weak she wasn't certain he could even hear her. But she saw him smile and run toward her. To him, a living one, she looked like a frail, naked old woman, collapsed in a lump against a desolate landscape.

"Abigail!" He nearly burst into tears when he saw her emaciated features. If this was death, it was indeed worse than anything he could have imagined.

He cradled her in his arms and she basked in his psychic energies, allowing herself a moment's respite before attempting to communicate further. He seemed to understand her need to gather strength from him.

In a way, she was stealing some of his psychic strength, just as Sanders was draining hers. But she knew he was young and had it to spare. She was an old, old spirit with no chance to save anyone unless she could rebuild her strength.

At last, she felt able to communicate. She told him of her awful dilemma, but did not describe the way in which Sanders's soul had melded with a force even more evil than his own, or that the two were even now horribly close by. She was certain it would frighten the boy away, and that would accomplish nothing.

"What can I do?" he asked softly.

"Be brave," she said. "Wait until the time is right, when the forces of good surround you. And then," she smiled, "let him have it with both barrels!"

"I don't understand," Paul said.

Abigail felt her strength weakening, and sensed Sanders awakening.

"Leave me now. Do as I say, or he'll steal your soul as well." It took all her might to kiss his cheek.

Paul stood on shaky legs and retreated into the mists.

"I'll be back," he said. "I promise."

Chapter Thirty-seven

"There's a million fruitcakes out there, and you had to run into one of them."

Lieutenant Hector Alvarez took another puff from his Marlboro and blew smoke toward the Silvers, seated across from his desk.

Louis Silver rubbed the smoke out of his eyes and said, "Did you question him? Are you sure . . ."

"Sure of what, Mr. Silver? Sure that he isn't a hired KGB hitman out to murder a nice Jewish family in town from . . ." he consulted a notepad for a moment. "From Rochester, New York? Yes, I'm sure, Mr. Silver."

Louis averted Alvarez's gaze, feeling humiliated. Alvarez was right. Since his experience with Dr. Sanders, Louis had been decidedly paranoid.

"The guy has a clean record. He won't say anything. My guess? He was probably looking for money for his next fix." Alvarez shrugged. "He overpowered the guard and was probably going to try and kidnap your son for ransom money. It happens, even here in the nation's capital. Don't let it spoil your vacation, Mr. Silver."

"I . . . I'd like to speak with the man," Louis stammered. "Why?"

"I don't know," he answered honestly. "I just . . ."

"Are you hiding something from me, Mr. Silver? Hmm?" Alvarez leaned across the desk until the cigarette threatened to burn a hole in Silver's nose.

"No, of course not. We'll be on our way now." Louis

stood up and motioned for Virginia and Paul to do the same.

As the group left the office, Alvarez called after them. "How much longer will you be here in Washington, Mr. Silver?"

For reasons he could not explain, Louis lied. "We're leaving tomorrow afternoon." He hoped Alvarez did not see his wife's expression of surprise. She knew their return tickets were for a flight later that day.

Once the Silvers had left, Alvarez went to the cell where the assailant was being held. He unlocked the door and motioned for the prisoner to follow him. When the two were alone in an empty questioning room, Alvarez grabbed the man by the shirt lapels.

"You fucked up," he screamed.

Though much bigger than Alvarez, the prisoner seemed genuinely frightened.

"You've got one more chance, asshole. This time, do not fuck up or you are dead meat. Got that?"

The man nodded fiercely, sweat beads flying off his bobbing head.

Alvarez stood up. "Now get the fuck out of here and wait for my call."

Alvarez escorted the man past the front desk and watched him leave, thinking that he would have to have him killed. The Big Man didn't tolerate failure, and now the heat would be on Alvarez to finish the botched job.

Alvarez hated to get personally involved in these things. He'd worked long and hard to get to his current position with the Washington police force. But some things were more important.

Like keeping the Big Man happy.

Chapter Thirty-eight

Louis slammed down the phone receiver in the hotel room. Virginia jumped nervously. "What's wrong?" she asked.

Louis pointed out the hotel window at a blanket of fog. "Airports closed. No flights in or out. They don't expect the fog to lift until tomorrow. We've been rebooked."

Virginia came to her husband's side, stroked his cheek. "Relax, honey. What's one day?"

Louis smiled, proud of his wife's resiliency. Just last night she'd cried herself to sleep, and now she was being the rock of the relationship. Louis had no idea how he'd live without his wife.

Within a day, that question would come back to haunt him.

Paul was dreaming. He was back home, in bed, sheets pulled over his head. He heard the doorbell ringing downstairs. No one seemed to be answering it.

Paul arose as he heard someone banging a fist against the door. Who . . . ?

"Mom?"

No one home but him. Where was everyone?

He stumbled downstairs, rubbing his eyes. He felt drugged.

The knocking persisted. He raised a sluggish arm to the doorknob, twisted it and opened the door.

Before him stood Abigail Alio.

Paul blinked in disbelief. "You're dead!"

Her mouth formed words he could not hear.

"What? Speak louder. Abigail, what's wrong?" He reached out to touch her but his hands went right through her shoulders. She disappeared and Paul awoke.

In his street clothes, wearing dark sunglasses, Hector Alvarez looked like any tourist. He made his way through the lobby of the Marbury House, suitcase in hand, with no interruptions.

Upstairs, he knocked on the door of the room next to the Silver's. There was no answer. He used a trick key and quickly entered the empty room.

He leaned his head against the connecting doorway, and could hear Louis speaking with his wife on the other side. He smiled and went back to the suitcase he'd left on the bed. He opened it and played with the timer that was attached to the dozen sticks of dynamite inside the suitcase.

When he heard the satisfying sound of the ticking, he left the room. Following the Big Man's orders, Alvarez had already eliminated the guy who'd botched the Silver termination. And now Alvarez figured that, by the time the explosion blew the Silvers to kingdom come, he'd be back at his office.

Jarred Hastings sat behind his desk and stared at the painting of grazing cows that adorned an office wall. He'd purchased the painting to remind himself that most people were like cows: pleasant, stupid beasts who existed to be used by those smarter.

Hastings recalled his first phone conversation with the reporter, Hamilton, regarding the Silver boy. Hastings's initial reaction was to dismiss Hamilton as a crank. But when Hamilton had mentioned Joe Simmons, Hastings's heart had begun to race.

It had been almost two decades since Hastings had assassinated his presidential opponent. Then came the rude surprise, as Simmons's brother, a popular senator from New Hampshire, had announced his presidential candidacy on his brother's behalf, and gone on to win.

The defeat would have been enough to drive a normal man crazy, Hastings thought. But he was anything but normal, and anything but crazy. Obsessed, yes; that he would admit. Hastings was obsessed with the thought of how one man could change the world.

It had happened before. Genghis Khan had nearly conquered the world. So had Napoleon, to say nothing of Hitler.

For a long time, Hastings had felt that America had been sliding downhill into a morass of pacifistic policies that would surely lead to a failed confrontation with the Soviets.

It had been this fear, early in his political career, that had helped Hastings decide to run for the presidency. And when the Republicans had made Hastings their candidate in 1968, it appeared his goal was going to be met. Only Joe Simmons stood in his way.

Joe Simmons had been the leading proponent of the fairy-tale, laissez-faire policies that were leading America down a garden path to hell. It would take a strong, brave man to stand in the face of Simmons's charisma and wrest control of the country back to those who knew best how to keep it free.

The problem was, the people of America were easily led—by Simmons's good looks, by his charisma, by a clever PR campaign. The future of the American way of life was just too damned important to allow it to fall to ruin just because the people of America could not see past Simmons's hype.

Hastings was not about to let the cows, as he privately referred to the voting public, decide which man was going to direct the country for the next four critical years. So he'd hired a mercenary who tailed Simmons for months, awaiting the perfect opportunity to kill the candidate without arousing any suspicions of a political assassination.

When Simmons and his wife had announced their annual vacation to Cape Cod, Hastings's hired killer had firmed up his plan. Simmons was a well-known exercise freak who always started his day with a swim. The killer, well trained in scuba diving, would be invisible underwa-

ter, yet close enough to locate Simmons from below and
fatally wound him with a poison-tipped spear.

Simmons had become anxious when, on the agreed day
of death, his hired man had lost Simmons in the murky
waters of the Atlantic. But the second time had worked
without a hitch. Simmons's dead body had been weighted
down and left for the fish, and had his body ever been
found, the autopsy would have shown a fatal dose of
poison from a rare jellyfish. From his safe perch on the
shoreline, Hastings had spotted his man through binocu-
lars, waving a high sign.

Hastings had rewarded the killer by getting him a job
with the Washington police force, and making certain he
was promoted regularly. Now, twenty years later, Hector
Alvarez was a respected lieutenant in the Washington police
department. And he was still on Hastings's payroll.

And, while Hastings was not satisfied with Alvarez's
performance over the past few days, he was still a necessary means to an end. That end, Hastings ruminated, was
freedom for America. Freedom from foreign aggression,
from reliances on foreign oil, from the whims of twisted
Communist leaders who were out to destroy America.

Hastings knew that he would not be a popular president.
He was a hawk in a generation of doves. But he saw
clearly that it would take a nuclear skirmish to teach the
Russians and the world's other Communists and terrorists
that America meant business again. Millions of lives could
afford to be lost if, in the process, America could regain
its lost greatness. It was not such a terrible price to pay.

It was all possible—but only if Hastings first reached
the White House. Then, before Congress knew what was
happening, he could declare martial law, wrest control of
the government, and turn his full attention to conquering
the enemies of America.

It was all so close to reality that, even sitting behind his
sturdy oak desk, Hastings could almost feel the power he
would soon have as President of the United States, as ruler
of the New World that he would forge from the ashes of
the old.

It was all meant to be, Hastings was convinced. Ever

since he'd been a kid, he'd followed the voice in his head
that told him his mission in life and how to achieve it.
That voice had told him to assassinate Joseph Simmons
twenty years ago.

And it had told him that he see that Paul Silver and his
family never be allowed to tell their strange story to a
receptive audience.

And so, the voice told him, they must die. All of them,
even that fool reporter Martin Hamilton.

Hastings looked at his watch. By now, if that bastard
Alvarez had finally done his job correctly, they would
already be dead.

And at nearly that precise second, a suitcase of explosives erupted its contents angrily. The explosion could be
heard throughout Georgetown, the force of its detonation
blowing the entire third floor of the hotel to kingdom
come.

Chapter Thirty-nine

"Is everyone okay?" Louis Silver shouted as he regained his feet. He looked around at the hotel lobby, now a shambles of cracked plaster and shattered glass. Everywhere he looked, he saw the explosion's aftermath: people, some lying still, others shaking glass or plaster out of their hair. One of the hotel guests was moaning eerily, pulling a huge chunk of glass from his arm.

Virginia used Louis as a crutch to slowly rise on shaky legs. She hugged her husband desperately.

"Where's Paul?" she screamed, spotting him a moment later pushing an overturned chair off himself. By his side, Martin Hamilton was feeling his head for bruises.

Virginia rushed to Paul. "Are you all right, honey?" she asked. Paul nodded, but his eyes were glassy. Virginia hugged her son to her breast.

"My God, the boy was right," Hamilton said. "And if he hadn't warned us, we'd have been up there . . ." He raised his eyes to look at the gaping hole in the hotel lobby's ceiling.

"It wasn't me, it was Abigail," Paul said as he struggled to keep his balance. Louis cleared debris off a nearby sofa and Virginia placed Paul on its cushion. They watched him carefully as he closed his eyes, took several deep gulps of the dusty air, and then opened his eyes again.

"I'm okay now," he said shakily.

Louis's knees popped as he bent to Paul's eye level. "We owe you our lives," his father said.

Paul shook his head. "You owe Abigail."

He remembered awakening after his strange dream with the overwhelming urge to attempt communication with Abigail, Sanders or no. He'd put himself into a trance and she'd immediately appeared to him.

"Abigail!" He rushed to hug her but she pulled back.

"Danger," she said, her voice no more than a whisper. "Leave the room—leave the hotel! Now!"

"I don't understand . . ."

Paul was horrified that he could actually see through Abigail, her body a frail glass sculpture of a very, very old soul. Then, as suddenly as she'd appeared, she was gone. Paul, back to normal, bounded out of bed and into his parents' room. He'd screamed at them to leave the room, that there was danger there. He had to hope they would do as he said without asking questions. Fortunately they complied, running down the hotel corridors while still dressing, stopping at Hamilton's room just long enough to rouse him.

They'd just reached the hotel lobby when the explosion's concussion had sent them all sprawling.

Now, Paul faced his parents tearfully.

"She saved our lives," he said, "and now we have to save her soul!"

His father leaned in to address him softly. "Sparky, Abigail did a beautiful thing for us, but she knows it's impossible for us to help her. She doesn't want you to face Sanders again—none of us do. You could die—and that's not what she wants."

Martin Hamilton broke in. "Listen, we could all die. It's obvious that's what someone wants. We've got to get out of here—out of Washington."

"You're right, Martin," Louis said. "Let's get to the airport. We'll be safer there." He wiped some soot off his glasses and led his group toward the entranceway.

"What about our stuff?" Virginia asked.

"It's bound to be a total loss. We'll deal with it from

Rochester. Right now, it's more important that we get home."

Even as he said the words, Louis wondered whether, even in Rochester, they would be safe.

The Silvers sat huddled together in the backseat of the taxi while Hamilton rode shotgun with the cabdriver.

"Let's review the facts," Hamilton said, his reporter's antennae up.

Too exhausted to argue, Louis let the man have the podium.

"This police lieutenant . . . Alvarez, right? Either he's incredibly stupid or he's involved. But he has no reason to want to see us dead. He's obviously working for someone who does. But whom?"

Suddenly, Paul sat bolt upright. "We can't leave yet," he said. "What about Senator Hastings? His life is still in danger . . ."

Paul's father smiled down at his son. "I'd say we've done our share for Hastings. It's time to think of our own safety."

"Hastings," Martin said softly, stroking his day's growth of stubbly beard. "Paul, when you spoke with Joe Simmons, did he ever actually say that Hastings's life was in danger?"

Paul thought for a moment, then shrugged. "I can't remember. I think so."

There was a glint in Hamilton's eyes that Louis Silver had not noticed before.

"Is it possible, Paul, that Simmons was trying to warn you against Hastings? That maybe Hastings was the source of the danger?"

Louis interrupted. "What are you getting at, Martin?"

"What I'm suggesting," Hamilton spoke quickly, "is that Simmons was actually trying to say that Hastings was his killer."

"Why would he wait twenty years to tell us?" Virginia asked.

"Because," Louis guessed, "he needed someone with

Paul's power to come along, and then he had to wait until Paul could control it.''

Martin added, ''And if a killer is our next President, we'll really have something to worry about.''

The cabbie, a college-age kid with long hair and an earring, who had appeared to ignore his passengers till now, interjected, ''You ask me, Hastings is a right-wing lunatic fascist.''

Virginia shook her head. ''This is ridiculous. So what if we think Hastings is behind this? What are we going to do—walk up to the guy and tell him we're on to him? He'd have the FBI throw us in prison for the rest of our lives. Or worse. Besides, I'm not even sure I believe it.''

Everyone in the car fell silent except for the cabbie, who said, ''Airport's comin' up. What terminal?''

Hamilton looked behind the cab for any suspicious vehicles. If he was right, and Hastings was out to kill them, would he really let them leave Washington alive?

Chapter Forty

Hastings was livid. An hour ago, Alvarez had phoned to admit that the hotel bombing had not done its job. Not only were the Silvers and Martin Hamilton safe and sound, but Alvarez had traced them to Washington National Airport, where they were waiting to board a flight back to Rochester.

That left Hastings with very little time to do what he should have done all along: to arrange their killings personally.

Virginia pulled Louis aside at the crowded airline gate where the family waited to board their flight.

"This won't work," she said. "Running won't solve anything. We have to confront Hastings. Tell him what we know, and tell him Hamilton will print what he's learned if Hastings doesn't give himself up."

Louis shook his head. "We're jumping at shadows. We haven't a shred of proof against him. Hamilton would have to be crazy to go out on a limb by writing up our side of the story. And even if he did, his editor would never allow the article to see print."

A loudspeaker announcement startled Louis into silence. "Would Mr. Louis Silver please pick up a white courtesy telephone? Mr. Louis Silver . . ."

Hesitantly, Louis approached the nearby white phone on the wall and picked it up.

"Hello?"

"Mr. Silver! I'm so glad I caught you in time!"

Alvarez! Louis regarded the phone receiver as if it were about to bite him. It took all of his strength to reposition the phone over his ear.

". . . were right! I had the FBI check out your story, and they found the man who tried to have you killed. He's admitted everything." The excited voice took a breath. "Mr. Silver? Are you there?"

Like a man being pulled inexorably toward the edge of a cliff, Louis Silver answered, "Yes, I'm here."

"The FBI needs corroboration from you to hold the bastard. I'm coming by to pick you up. I'll arrange a later flight for you. Is that all right?"

"I . . . guess so." Maybe Alvarez was telling the truth. Maybe the FBI had really done its job for a change. Maybe their troubles were over.

Or maybe he was pushing himself and his family over that cliff and straight down to hell.

Louis explained the call to his stunned family and Hamilton.

"It doesn't make any sense," the reporter complained loudly, fighting the loudspeaker message that was announcing boarding for their flight. "If the FBI wants to speak with us, why didn't the FBI contact us?"

"I think we're all being too paranoid," Louis countered, his brain awash in confused thoughts.

Virginia hugged her husband. "Honey, let's just go home. If the FBI wants to contact us there, they will."

Louis, his hands shaking, slowly nodded. "Okay. Let's go."

Using every ounce of her dwindling strength, Abigail focused on her captor. Sanders retained no resemblance to his once-human form. He was now a mass of twisting, slimy worms with hundreds of eyes and thousands of sucking appendages, all clinging to her, siphoning her very soul. Soon, she would be nonexistent, and the demon inside Sanders would be stronger than ever.

The Silvers had gathered their carry-on possessions and

were headed toward the boarding ramp when their path
was blocked by Hector Alvarez.

"I'm here—let's go," he smiled at them.

Louis shook his head. "We decided if the FBI wants us,
they can come to Rochester."

'I'm sorry, Mr. Silver, but you can't do that. The FBI
needs to speak with you, and if you won't come willingly,
they can have you . . . detained. Now let's not make a
scene. Come with me."

Louis turned to his wife. "Should we go?" Virginia
shrugged. "What do you say, Martin?"

"I say we stay—and that everything that happens to us
sees print once I reach Rochester." The reporter smiled
insidiously at Alvarez.

"No problem, sir. We have nothing to hide. Now, if
you'll follow me . . . ?"

Chapter Forty-one

"I should have known," Louis chided himself. He wanted more than anything to reach across to the car's front seat and wrap his hands around Alvarez's neck. But Louis's hands were handcuffed behind his back.

"Like they say in the movies," Martin Hamilton said, "you'll never get away with this."

Alvarez laughed. "You're dead meat and you want me to worry!"

"Shut up, Alvarez," Hastings snarled.

"So it was all a lie," Hamilton continued. "The story about the FBI catching our mysterious assailant . . . everything." The reporter struggled but was unable to maneuver his manacled hands.

"If I'm not on that plane," Hamilton warned, "my editor's gonna raise hell till he finds out where I am. And what about the Silvers here? You think they can just disappear without friends and relatives notifying the authorities?"

Hastings smiled, looking past Silver at the Washington skyline. "You used a good word, Hamilton: disappear. Because that's what you're all going to do. And there's not a chance in hell that you'll ever be found."

"But why, Hastings?" Louis asked. "Why would a man with so much to gain risk it all to see that a family from Anytown USA and a reporter get wiped off the face of the map? It just doesn't make sense."

"Well, Mr. Silver," Hastings replied, "I'm genuinely

211

sorry you have to be killed. I really am. But I can't afford to have anyone else hear that story about Paul's conversation with Mr. Simmons. And the way I understand it, the only people who know about that are right here in this car." He shrugged his shoulders. "It's just fate, I guess."

Next to him, Louis could feel his son shivering in fear. He wanted so much to be able to cradle Paul in his arms, but the damned handcuffs kept him at bay. "It's okay, Paul," he whispered, but Louis could see that the fear in Paul's eyes could not be assuaged by lies.

Louis had really blown it this time—gotten his family into a terminal jam. He was too depressed to look at his wife, who sat quietly, biting at her lip, looking out the window. Louis glanced out the window of the speeding patrol car, spotting Arlington National Cemetery, where endless rows of white crosses littered the landscape.

"Tell me, Alvarez," Louis said, "how many men and women have you killed by just following this madman's orders? How many children?"

Alvarez just sneered.

Paul winced. If it weren't for his "gift," they wouldn't be in this mess. And Hazel might not be dead. Maybe Johnny Richardson would still be alive . . .

"Where are we headed, Hastings?" Hamilton asked.

"Someplace quiet and secluded. Very appropriate, really," he laughed. The car turned in to the gates of Arlington Cemetery and was waved to a stop by a guard.

Hastings whispered, "This gun is aimed through the seat at your son. One word and he's dead."

"Dead now or dead an hour from now, what's the difference?" Hamilton muttered.

"Martin, please do as he says," Virginia said.

"Smart dame," Alvarez said.

"Afternoon, sir," the young guard addressed Hastings. "Here to visit your father, sir?"

"That's right, son."

"He was a great man, sir. One of my dad's idols during World War II."

Hastings cut him off. "Let us through, son."

The guard, barely out of his teens, flushed with embarrassment and saluted Hastings. "Yes, sir." He opened the employee gate and the Lincoln Continental whisked by him, throwing dust in his face. But the guard didn't care. He was a big fan of Hastings, whom he'd met many times before. The presidential candidate's limousine, with its darkened windows, was a familiar sight at the cemetery, where Hastings often came to visit his father's crypt.

"How come there's no other cars?" Paul asked, as their car rolled past endless rows of concrete slabs and white crosses.

"Cars are not allowed in the cemetery," Hastings answered absently. "With certain exceptions, of course."

"They don't wanna disturb the tenants," Alvarez said, breaking into his laughing squeal again.

The beefy-faced politician just smiled broadly. "We're here," he announced.

The car rolled to a stop before the entranceway to a huge marble crypt. On its immense marble door was a carving of General Eric Hastings in his full battle regalia.

"Lovely, isn't it?" Hastings asked. "So peaceful . . . so quiet. No one ever comes to this end of the park. It's not on the tour bus route, you see."

Virginia's stomach flipflopped. "You mean to kill us and leave our bodies in the crypt, don't you, you bastard?"

Hastings ignored her, turning his attention to Alvarez. "Make sure there's no one around, and then open the crypt," he snarled.

"This is grotesque," Martin Hamilton said. "It's a travesty of everything your father stood for . . ."

Hastings turned around in his seat, his face red. "On the contrary, Mr. Hamilton. My father and I are both freedom fighters, using all means at our disposal to see that the United States remains invincible. If, along the way, some peace-loving civilians become victims, well, one must keep in mind the greater good of the country."

Hastings looked around. There was no one in sight. The entire landscape was made up of white crosses. "These men," he said, waving at the markers, "were true patriots, giving up their lives to keep this country free. And that's what you'll be doing."

"Bullshit," Hamilton grunted.

"All clear," Alvarez said, poking his head through the passenger window on Hastings's side.

"My God, Hastings," Hamilton continued. "These men died fighting to save the world from fascist madmen like you."

"Would you help our guests, please?" Hastings said.

"Hastings," Louis said, "don't do this—not here. Lord, man, veterans from the Revolutionary War are here. Fallen soldiers from God knows how many wars. This is the final resting place of Robert and John Kennedy. What you're doing is blasphemy."

The candidate ordered Alvarez to lead the group inside the tomb. The police lieutenant hesitated a moment, pondering Hamilton's remarks, then shrugged. He was a team player, and Hastings was captain of the winning team.

Hastings slammed the immense door shut, plunging the crypt into darkness. Alvarez flicked on a flashlight, its harsh beam illuminating a huge marble sarcophagus that dominated the center of the room.

"Hard to breathe," Virginia said, coughing for air.

"It's airtight in here," Hastings explained. "Keeps the bugs away. That's the way Dad would have wanted it."

Paul screamed.

Alvarez trained the flashlight on the boy just in time to see him slip to the floor.

"What's wrong with him?" Alvarez asked, pointing the flashlight with one hand and his gun with another.

"What difference does it make?" Hastings said brusquely. "Kill them all. I'll be waiting in the car."

The politician backed out of the flashlight's gleam. Seconds later, a door slammed.

"Jesus, we're gonna die in here," Hamilton choked. The reality of his predicament was finally settling in.

"Shut up, Martin," Louis hissed. "You're wasting air." Louis ran an index finger along Paul's neck, checking for a pulse. It was alarmingly slow. Louis bent his head to listen for Paul's breath. It was nearly indistinguishable.

"What's wrong with him?" the reporter asked.

Though he said nothing, Louis was certain Paul had gone into a trance.

Chapter Forty-two

Hastings smiled as he locked the crypt's entrance. Now, no one could get out, including that bumbling idiot Alvarez. It was time for him to die as well. The air wouldn't last more than fifteen minutes, less if they screamed for help.

Let them scream, Hastings thought as he climbed into the limousine and started the engine. The crypt, he knew, was soundproof.

The limo approached the pesky young guard at the employee gate. Hastings slowed but did not open the window. From the outside, there was no way to see into the car.

The guard smiled and waved him on. The fool.

The senator looked at his watch. He had a press conference to attend in less than an hour. And it provided a perfect alibi for his whereabouts for the day, if necessary. He looked at himself in the rearview mirror and shuddered. Someone in the backseat?

"Dad?" he whispered.

The seat was empty. But just for the slightest moment, Hastings could have sworn he'd seen his father, dressed in his battle garb, stern disapproval etched across his strong features.

Nerves. That's all. Hastings laughed and turned his mind to the campaign speech he would be making in an hour to a nationwide TV audience. It was his last speech before the elections, and he intended to leave a lasting impression that would carry the voters of America into the poll booths like docile cows, his name cemented in their minds.

For it was Jarred Hastings's destiny to become the next President of the United States. He was certain, because the Voice had told him.

And the Voice never lied.

It was a different feeling this time, Paul thought as he fell into his trance. For starters, it had come unexpectedly, not at his bidding. He'd been pulled into it like a child being drawn into the ocean, where riptides of psychic energy had grabbed hold of him and sucked him into their depths. He was entirely out of control of the trance, being carried along by the psychic strength of someone—or some thing else.

He felt like he was traveling at the speed of light, and indeed the shapes around him were whizzing by so quickly that he could make out no details, just blurs of color, suggestions of shapes.

He fought to maintain consciousness, fearing that to give in to sweet oblivion would be fatal in some way even worse than death.

Or was he dead already? Paul looked around, trying to get his bearings. He was lying in a cavern of sorts, on a gray floor that was moist and spongy. The walls and ceiling were made of the same dead-gray material, all sticky and dripping with transparent, mucouslike material.

From behind, he heard a noise like a snake's hissing. The hackles rose on the back of his neck as Paul turned slowly around.

He was greeted by the twisted smile of Dr. Michael Sanders.

It was time to get this over with, Alvarez thought. This place gave him the willies. Already it seemed to be getting difficult to breathe, and Alvarez was sweating like a pig.

"Get away from the kid," Alvarez growled.

"My son is sick," Virginia screamed.

"Yeah? Well, that beats you, lady—you're dead." Alvarez pulled the trigger and Virginia jumped like a marionette. She landed with a heavy thud against Paul's chest. A small red circle appeared on Virginia's blouse.

"You fucking bastard!" Louis shouted, literally flying through the air and landing on the police lieutenant's shoulders, bringing them both down to the cold stone floor. Taken by surprise, Alvarez was unprepared to defend himself from the maddened Silver, who slammed the gunman's hand against the floor repeatedly until the weapon fell free. Martin Hamilton grabbed the Magnum, bringing it to rest against Alvarez's forehead.

"Hold very still," Hamilton said, "or I'll use this."

Alvarez stopped struggling. Louis disengaged himself and stood up. "Shoot him!" he shouted. "Like he shot Ginny! Shoot the motherfucker!" Louis attempted to grab the gun from Martin, who stood back.

"Get ahold of yourself, man!" Hamilton panted, short of breath. "I'll watch him—you check your wife."

Louis ran to Virginia's side. "Ginny," he cried as he felt her blood flowing into his hands. The wound was directly over her heart.

"Is she breathing?" Hamilton yelled.

Louis placed his ear directly over his wife's mouth and felt a tiny stream of warm air. "Just barely. We've got to get out of here! Get her to a hospital . . ."

His gun still trained on the cowering Alvarez, Martin backed to the crypt's door. He shoved against it but it didn't budge. He pushed harder to no avail.

"Where's the key to this place?" Hamilton yelled to Alvarez.

Surprise registered on Alvarez's sweaty face. "He wouldn't lock me in."

"Guess again, asshole," Hamilton grunted as he shoved backwards against the door with all his might. "I'll bet he's not even out there, you little shit. He's probably laughing all the way back to Washington about how he got rid of all of us at once. After all, he doesn't need you anymore. You've done your job, you slimy little shit."

Hamilton backed away from the door. He pointed the gun at the lock and fired. The noise in the crypt was deafening. The reporter rushed to the door, but the bullet barely dented the marble slab, and the lock was intact.

"Jesus," Alvarez whined, "we're all gonna die in here."

Chapter Forty-three

Was it really Sanders facing Paul? The boy wasn't certain. Somehow, Sanders's face was changing, subtly but perceptibly, all the time, as if it weren't a face at all, but a mass of maggots, ever-moving to form an obscene parody of facial features.

It was too hideous to watch. Paul turned away and his eyes opened even wider as he spotted Abigail Alio against a wet wall, her body barely more than a dried-up, transparent husk.

At first, Paul was too horrified by the sight to notice that Abigail was attempting to speak to him.

". . . the devil," she whispered.

Paul looked back at Sanders, more horrified than ever. The devil! And indeed Sanders now wore the fangs of a canine, and his eyes were slanted, snakelike slits. And even as Paul watched, the obscene transformation continued. The nose was now more piglike than human, the arms grew fur, the legs bent in on themselves, once at the knee and again at mid-calf. From between his legs wound a shiny, pointed tail.

"What? What did he say?" Louis gasped as he cradled his wife's head in his lap. She was barely breathing.

"I think he said, 'the devil,' " Martin stammered as he kept his attention on Alvarez.

Alvarez was becoming bolder, believing Hamilton too exhausted and shocked to shoot him. Already the police officer had inched his way to within a yard of Hamilton.

219

Alvarez knew he could kick the gun out of the reporter's hands the next time the man's attention was diverted. Then he'd kill them all and keep firing the gun at the door until he broke the lock or attracted attention from outside.

And he swore to himself that the next person he would kill would be Jarred Hastings.

In a wink of an eye, Sanders's tail disappeared. Now the body was normal, but the face was changing again.

"Who . . . are you?" Paul asked. His breath formed streams in the air. "Where's Sanders?"

"Sanders is . . . inside me," the creature answered in a mocking, half-speed parody of Sanders's own voice.

And then the clothing and the face changed again. It was an unfamiliar face to Paul, who had never seen a photo of Lee Harvey Oswald. A rifle had materialized in the man's hands, pointed at Abigail's head.

"Don't shoot!" Paul screamed and ran through the slush at his feet toward Abigail. Before he could reach her, Sanders was changing again, the firearm disappearing, replaced by a chain saw. The face above it was blood-spattered, missing teeth.

"Ed Gein's here, too," a chilling voice with a southern accent said. But already the face had remolded itself, and the Nazi uniform had appeared. "Alfred Goebbels," he said.

Another change. An older man this time, in a priest's habit. "Jim Jones."

A squat man in a suit and tie with a carnation popping out of a bullet hole in his chest. "Al Capone."

An effete little mustached man in an out-of-date suitcoat. "John Wilkes Booth."

The transformations were happening at lightning speed. Paul closed his eyes, threw his hands over his ears, until at last there was silence.

He opened one eye. Before him was a nightmare in red. It was, Paul realized, a man whose skin had been peeled away to reveal the bloodied musculature beneath. Atop the terrifying body was a shiny white skull. Somehow, the mouth opened and Paul heard it say, "I am evil. I am your adversary.

Welcome to Hell.''

Virginia could see her own body, laid out some ten feet beneath her, cradled in her husband's arms. She saw her son laying on the cold stone floor close to her own body. Martin Hamilton was feeling for the boy's pulse with one trembling hand while with the other he trained a gun on Alvarez.

And then, maddeningly, the scene faded into complete darkness as Virginia felt herself moving at impossible speed. Before she had time to panic, she spotted her destination, at first nothing more than a tiny pinprick of light that must have been a thousand miles away. And yet, in the blink of an eye the light had advanced upon her and enveloped her in comforting warmth.

"I am the voice that spoke to Sanders," the demon hissed. "I speak to Hastings even now. Great men and little men. And little children as well," the creature said, leering at Paul.

"Is everyone bad . . . possessed?" Paul choked.

"Those who aren't derive their power from those who are. Those who are get their strength from me," the demon said, poking a five-inch fingernail into its chest, bringing forth a tiny trickle of yellow blood. "Do you want to share that strength?" it leered.

Paul's attention was diverted by a groan from Abigail, whose still form was beginning to shimmer and fade from sight. Paul knew instinctively that in moments she would cease to exist on this or any other plane.

"Why?" Paul screamed. "Why are you torturing Abigail?"

The demon laughed, the sound a grotesque cross between a child's scream of terror and an animal's grunt of ecstasy. It extended an impossibly long arm toward Paul, who skittered backward on his hands and knees.

"She means nothing to me," the beast declared. "Just a means to an end. Yours."

The beast's fingertip touched Paul and the boy hissed in pain. It felt like he'd been branded.

"It's you I want, boy," the demon hissed. "I used her,

and Sanders, and even your friend Johnny, to draw you to me.''

"But why? Why me?'' Paul cried.

The devil regarded Paul as if he were a lab specimen under a microscope. "Each millenium a child is born with special powers. I felt it in you as you were born, shining like a beacon. I saw it being nurtured as you suckled at your mother's breast, sensed it exploding as the child became a boy and the boy a young man. By that time, my agents were in place.''

The demon counted claws on one hand. "Sanders . . . Hastings . . . Filippo . . . yes, and even your best friend, Johnny! I needed them to bring you to me.''

Paul shook his head. It was too much to comprehend. "What do you want with me?''

The demon screamed, "Hell is not enough! I grow weary of manipulating others from afar. I crave more power. Your power. It courses through your veins like a mighty, untapped river. I will control you, piglet, use your psychic energy to return to earth. In your body,'' it sneered.

Paul felt himself starting to lose his grip on reality. He doubted that all of his so-called psychic powers could win against the terrible thing that stood before him.

Paul retreated mentally, to an earlier, easier time. In his mind's eye, he was two years old, back in his crib, having a terrifying nightmare. If only he could wake up and call for his mother.

"Mommy!'' Paul screamed, as the demon bellowed its obscene laugh.

Chapter Forty-four

"Mommy!"

His cry seemed to come from inside her own head, but Virginia was prompted to turn away from the warm, peaceful light and look back toward the darkness.

Paul! Her son was in mortal danger! Virginia willed herself to his side, and in a moment, was there. She stood protectively between Paul's prone form and a terrifying creature.

"No!" she screamed, eyes wide, nostrils flaring, hands held out protectively against the horrifying shape before her. Her fingers felt like they were on fire as a ball of sparkling energy emerged from her fingertips, melding into a pencil-thin laser bolt of energy. The white line of light, so bright that Virginia was forced to look away, shot straight into the demon's shoulder, which boiled and pussed as the creature hissed in pain.

"S . . . stay away from him!" she screamed, not knowing what was happening or how she had found such psychic strength. To her amazement, the demon-thing stopped in its tracks, and a moment later, she was facing her own husband.

"Lou? Louis? I . . . don't understand."

"Honey," he said, arms open wide, "It's all right. You were shot and you were hallucinating. But it's all right now. Everything is fine. Come here."

She felt her grip on reality slipping. "Your arm is bleeding," she said.

"I was shot," Louis smiled. "But I'm fine, really I am. Come here, honey."

"Mom, no!" Paul screamed. "It's not Dad—it's the devil!"

For a moment, the image before her shimmered like someone seen through a waterfall, and then it was her husband again.

"Paul, don't confuse your mother. She's still in shock from being shot. I'm trying to help her. Come here, honey."

Paul rose to his hands and knees and scrambled forward until he'd struck the back of his mother's legs, sending her tumbling. "Mom, he's not what you think he is. He's the devil!"

Virginia groaned in terror. Was she already dead, she wondered, and was this her own private hell—to have to watch her son threatened by this monstrous beast?

Paul cried, "I need your help, Mom."

"Don't listen to him," the beast scowled.

"He used Abigail to bring me to him, and now he's going to use my powers to cross over to earth."

"But why?" Virginia asked, struggling to maintain her sanity in this scene from a horror film in which she somehow was playing a lead role.

The devil's eyes seemed to bore through to her very soul and Virginia shrank away from that obscene gaze.

"I will be the nexus of all evil," it said, "a black hole for man's basest instincts. And I've already picked my host—your son."

"Five minutes, sir," the studio page alerted Hastings, who was sitting in a director's chair while a makeup artist expertly erased his crow's-feet and gave him a smooth tan.

"Good luck, sir," the makeup girl offered shyly.

Hastings just smiled.

Alvarez took advantage of the momentary confusion in the crypt to lunge at the gun dangling from Hamilton's hand. Seeing something out of the corner of his eye, and acting on reflex, Hamilton brought the gun up, slamming it into Alvarez's groin. The man howled in pain and fell to the floor. Hamilton brought the gun butt down hard against the side of Alvarez's skull. He twitched and lay still.

"Is he dead?" asked Louis dully.

Martin realized Louis was in shock. The reporter shook his head. "I don't think so. How is Virginia?"

"I can't feel a pulse," Louis cried. "I think she's gone."

Hamilton turned away, leaving the man some privacy for his grief. He gazed at Paul and was shocked to see that the boy was trying to speak. Martin bent to hear what he was saying.

"Mom, help me," Paul whimpered.

"Give me your hand, Paul," Virginia whispered. The boy grabbed his mother's outstretched hand and immediately felt stronger.

Virginia was suddenly clear-headed. She knew instinctively what she had to do.

"We can beat it, Paul," Virginia said loudly, not caring if the demon heard her. Hoping, in fact, that it did. "We will beat it."

Chapter Forty-five

"How can we help? What can we do?" Hamilton gasped. It was almost impossible to breathe in the airtight crypt. Even his sweat, Hamilton noted absently, had evaporated.

Louis looked at his wife's still form and then to his son, whose body was twitching like he was receiving electroshock treatment. It was a scene from hell.

Finally, he turned his tearing gaze to the reporter and whispered, "Pray."

Paul's mother held her son against her bosom. "Listen to me, Paul. Martin said something back in the crypt—that there are many good men buried in Arlington. Can you feel their spirits? Are they still on this plane? Can they help us now?"

"Your mother is crazy, Paul," the demon sneered. "Don't listen to her." But he held back, as if approaching the embraced duo was painful.

Virginia continued, trying to ignore the beast's taunts. "Can you feel them, Paul? Are they there? Open up to them, Paul."

Paul stared at the demon-beast, petrified. "If I use my power," he whimpered, "it'll get me."

"That's right, Paul," the devil said. "I'll get you good."

Virginia shook her son's shoulders till he refocused on her. "Don't listen to it. It's trying to confuse you. Listen to me. The spirits of the brave, good men buried here—reach out to them, Paul! They're our only chance!"

The demon's eyes flared. "Reach out to me!" it hissed. His forked tongue flitted from between his fangs, dripping sticky green mucus.

Paul shook his head violently. "I'm scared, I can't, don't make me! I'll die!"

"What's he saying?" Louis said softly, eyes still closed. He had actually been praying to a God he'd never had use for until now.

Martin rushed to Paul's side. "He's saying he's scared, that he can't do it! That he's going to die! What the hell's going on inside his head?"

Louis clenched his fists so hard he could feel his fingernails piercing his skin. "Paul!" he screamed. "We're here! We won't let you die!"

Chapter Forty-six

The beast became Sanders again, this time its face decomposing, one eyeball hanging by a thread. Paul turned away in disgust and terror.

"It wants to frighten you, Paul," Virginia said, standing her ground between the boy and the thing. "To keep you from using your power."

"I'm scared, Mom!" Paul yelled, and a moment later the twisted thing had shimmered and shapechanged into a mirror image of Paul himself, one that echoed Paul's words.

"I'm scared, Mom!" it said, and in a moment of dizzy disbelief, Virginia couldn't tell which was her son.

"Help me, Mom! Hold me!" one of the boys cried.

She had to restrain herself from going to him, from enfolding him in her arms. She knew that to voluntarily go to the beast would put her in its power forever—like a victim inviting the embrace of a psychic vampire.

"Mom, I need you!" the boy screamed, eyes red with tears.

"Paul," she called out in exasperation, "it's scared of us! Don't you see? That's why it won't attack. You're too powerful. You can beat it, Paul, you can!"

One of the boys fell silent while the other continued to scream and beg for his mother. But which was which?

"It's not working," Hamilton gasped.

"Shut up," Louis screamed, shaking the reporter by the

229

shoulders. Martin lost his balance and fell to his hands and knees.

"I'm dizzy," he said absently.

Louis dropped to his hands and knees as well. "Martin, please, for God's sake—for Paul's sake, don't give up on him. Pray!"

Louis stared down at his wife's peaceful face and admitted to himself that he didn't even know how to pray. He'd just been sitting there for the last ten minutes feeling sorry for Paul, for Virginia, but most of all, for himself.

"God, please," he thought, "I don't know how to say this. I've never felt I needed you before. I didn't even know if you existed. But I need you now, God. Please don't fail me. Show me the way to my son's side, so that I may give him my strength."

Unknowingly, Louis had begun to talk aloud to himself. At first, Martin ignored him, then he couldn't help but listen. Finally, the reporter joined Louis's side and placed an arm around the man.

"Repeat after me," Martin said softly. Louis, eyes blurred with tears, looked at Martin hopefully.

"Our Father, who art in Heaven, hallowed be thy name."

One Paul fell to his knees, pulling at his hair and shrieking.

The other closed his eyes and let the images flood into his brain. Before him stretched a multitude of faces. There was a man in a blue uniform, and one in gray, a third in khaki, all little more than fuzzy blurs, yet everyone offering his hand in gestures of help and strength.

Men in tattered soldiers' uniforms from a half-dozen wars, women in nursing garb— They surrounded Paul, these brave young men and women who had died in endless battles and forgotten conflicts. Some carried muskets, others bayonets. Some carried weapons he couldn't even recognize. On some, Paul smelled fear, but in all of them, Paul could feel the bravery, shining like beacons in the darkest night.

Their strength was quickly rebuilding Paul's own. He felt like a human pincushion as the soldiers' psychic energy flooded into each one of his pores. Far from painful, the effect was incredibly rejuvenating.

The energy was immense, and soon there was too much of it to contain in his own body. Paul felt excess psychic energy oozing out of his pores in a white mist that began to harden into a protective bubble around himself and his mother.

The demon resumed its own shape, laughing. "Not enough," he screamed. "Your power is still not equal to my own! I, too, have my reinforcements!" The beast reached out, embracing the space around him, drawing strength from discarnate evil spirits.

Grinning wickedly, the demon pointed at the bright white bubble surrounding Paul and his mother and tweaked a black ball of energy from his fingertips. It impacted with the white bubble and cracked its surface, knocking Paul off his feet.

"You can't win," the demon yelled at Paul, who was struggling to regain his footing. "Not when I've chosen the battleground!"

For the first time, Paul saw the chamber they were in for what it truly was: the inside of a human brain.

The demonic beast's body shrank, adding the features and clothing of a young boy.

In front of Paul stood Johnny Richardson.

The brittle white protective bubble around Paul and his mother cracked into thousands of tiny pieces and disappeared into the ether.

"Our battle is over," the demon beast inside Johnny Richardson's body said. "Now, come to me."

Chapter Forty-seven

"Five seconds," the director announced.

Jarred Hastings checked his tie and smiled broadly into the camera.

"Four . . . three . . . two . . . one . . . on the air!"

Norm Wilson, the young, well-coiffed newscaster, announced, "Good evening, ladies and gentlemen, and welcome to *Meet Your Candidate*. Tonight, a candid conversation with the Republican Presidential nominee, Jarred Hastings. Good evening, sir." The two shook hands.

"Well, son, that's what I feel this country needs to get back on its feet—a firm grip on its problems and some no-nonsense solutions."

"What sort of problems are you most concerned with?"

Hastings smiled. "We're a country of cows, Mr. Nelson, without a shepherd. I intend to be that shepherd."

The program host looked up from his notes. "I beg your pardon? Is that a religious reference?"

Hastings laughed. "You could call it that."

"I didn't realize you were a spiritual person, Mr. Hastings. Do you believe in God?"

Hastings turned his smirk into a smile as it settled across his face. "Oh yes, I do. He guides my every move."

Paul couldn't believe his eyes. Before him stood Johnny Richardson.

"Johnny," Paul said weakly, "is . . . it really you?"

"It's me, asshole. And I'm finally gonna get you back for killing me."

"Johnny, it wasn't me who killed you. It was that creep, Vic. I told you he was no good—you wouldn't listen to me. You'd still be . . . still be alive if you'd listened to me, Johnny."

For a moment, Johnny's image shimmered, lost focus, and took on the form of the devil again. "You scared him away, piglet," growled the demon, waggling a claw at Paul. "Mustn't do that. Johnny is mine now, for all eternity. As is your precious Hazel."

Paul shook his head. "No," he said, his voice surprisingly calm. He managed to stare directly into the cat's eyes of the leering devil, addressing the friend whose soul was somehow locked inside that obscene form.

"Johnny," Paul started, "if you're . . . in there, listen to me. I want to free you and Abigail—to go on from here, to wherever it is you're supposed to go."

"Never," sneered the demon.

"I'm . . . not afraid to die," Paul said softly. "Not if it brings us together again, Johnny. As friends."

The devil, frothing from its foul-smelling mouth, advanced toward Paul, who slid backward on the moist fleshy ground.

"I miss you, Johnny."

Johnny shimmered back into view in place of the devil. "No," Johnny screamed, hands over his ears. "It's just more lies. Lies like the voice told me—the devil's voice! It said if I helped him, it would give me back my life!" Johnny broke down, crying in huge sobs. "It's so terrible here, Paul. I'm so scared!"

Johnny screamed in pain as his head split down the middle and the devil's red, bloody face emerged, swelling quickly to its full size.

"Enough," it bellowed. "You can't win, piglet. Now come to me. I'll make your death painless. I promise," he said with a leer.

"Like you promised Johnny?" Paul shouted. He glanced at Johnny's body on the floor, discarded like a snake's skin.

"Johnny was nothing, just another way to reach you. Your power is incredible. I need it . . . now!"

Paul stood up, finding new strength. "You should've never mentioned Johnny."

Paul grabbed his mother's hand, felt her strength adding measurably to his.

". . . thy kingdom come . . ."
"Thy kingdom come . . ."
". . . thy will . . . be done . . ."
"Thy will be done . . ."

Martin shook his head. "Can't talk . . . anymore . . . no air . . ."

Louis shook the reporter and they both fell to the floor, where they lay panting.

"Finish . . . it . . . you bastard," Louis wheezed. "For . . . Paul's sake . . . finish it!"

Martin attempted to swallow but there was no moisture left in his mouth. He coughed till it hurt. Finally, he fell silent again.

". . . yea," he whispered, "though we walk . . . through the valley . . . of the shadow . . . of death . . . I will fear no evil . . ."

And in that moment, Paul felt his strength multiplied a thousandfold. Around him, there was an endless sea of faces, some no more than skulls with patches of flesh and hair, urging him on.

Paul shivered as, in the throngs, he spotted a man who looked like the image carved on the door of the tomb. General Hastings! To his side was Abigail, her eyes bright, her smile radiant. And next to her, Johnny Richardson, whole again, and waving Paul on.

"For me," Paul heard the thought transmitted to him from the spirit of his best friend.

The spectral army spoke in unison: "For your country."

His mother whispered, "For your soul."

Paul clenched his fists and a white, protective aura immediately surrounded them. Paul could feel each part of his body becoming supercharged with spectral energy.

The demon before him pressed clawed hands to its forehead and called on the energies of the evil dead.

''Now!'' Paul yelled, releasing all his incredible energy in one ballooning burst of white light. Ten laser-brilliant streaks exploded from Paul's fingertips and struck the demon. Its form writhed like a creature being boiled in oil. Its features transformed a hundred times in seconds. The demon's form grew, shrank, changed clothing, lost arms and legs, grew hair and lost it, as it exorcised all of its ghostly hosts in one massive psychic overload.

Something inhuman shrieked in agony as Paul continued to direct the pencil-thin streaks of spectral energy into it, until the creature exploded into a hundred mini-fireballs that shot in all directions and disappeared moments later.

Hastings smiled at the camera. ''In formulating my philosophy,'' he said, ''every step of the way, I have asked for God's guidance. It is His will that guides me—I am just His instrument.''

A fireball of white light appeared from nowhere and shot into Hastings's open mouth. The man lit up like a Christmas ornament before his eyeballs exploded outward, followed by his entire skull.

''Jesus!'' Norm Wilson screamed.

The program director yelled, ''Get us off the air! Now!''

A fireball flew past the unconscious forms of Martin Hamilton and Louis Silver, impacting against the stone doors of the crypt, disintegrating them instantaneously and allowing sweet fresh air to flood the tomb.

The fireball flew back into the tomb where it expanded until it covered Hector Alvarez's body. As the fireball disintegrated in a shower of sparks, so did Alvarez.

Two fireballs struck the still form of Virginia Silver, one at her toes, the other at the crown of her head. The twin orbs of energy moved slowly toward each other, bathing her entire form in their spectral energy. They met over her heart, where they formed a whirlpool that disappeared into her bloody clothing. A moment later, a bullet flew out of her still form and disintegrated in the streaming light.

Once again, the crypt fell silent.

Chapter Forty-eight

Paul awoke in the misty spiritual environment.

Helping him to his feet was Johnny. And, standing next to him was Abigail. She glowed so brightly that Paul found it almost impossible to look straight at her. He ran toward her but she stretched a hand out to stop him, shaking her head, a sad smile on her face.

"I'm going on, Paul. To the next level. Be happy for me."

"I . . . I am. But I'll miss you."

With the last vestige of her physical form, she touched his mouth with her fingertips. He felt a million pinpricks of energy on his lips as she pulled her fingers away.

Just before she disappeared entirely, she relayed a final thought to Paul.

"We will meet again."

Then, she allowed her soul-self to loosen its stitches and unravel into the fabric of the universe.

Paul wiped tears from his eyes and faced Johnny.

"I'm so sorry," Johnny said. "For everything. I was weak, you see, and that . . . thing used me. For years. At first, I thought I was going crazy, and then I was crazy, I guess."

"Johnny . . ." Paul started. He didn't have the strength to continue.

"I have to be on my way now, too," his friend continued. "But I think I'll be around again. Maybe do better next time," he said with a wistful smile. "I hope so." He looked at Paul. "Do you forgive me?" he said softly.

"Of course." Paul ran forward and hugged his best friend.

After a moment, Johnny disappeared and Paul felt himself slip softly into the white mist, and then he felt nothing more.

Chapter Forty-nine

Paul awoke, shocked to see his mother cradling him in her arms. Just over her shoulder, his dad was smiling down at him. Nearby, Martin Hamilton brushed tears from his eyes.

A jeep pulled up at the crypt entrance, which had been completely disintegrated by the white light.

"What the hell's going on here?" the gate guard yelled as he stepped out of his vehicle.

"Not hell, son," Martin said softly. "Anything but hell."

"Are you really okay, Ginny?" Louis asked.

Virginia touched a sore spot above her heart. "Feels like I got kicked by a mule. But I'm all right. Somehow."

"Thank God," Louis whispered.

"Exactly," Martin Hamilton added.

Louis noticed Virginia staring at him incredulously.

"What's wrong?" he said. "What do you see?"

"It's you," she answered. "What do you see?"

"I don't understand," he said. Rubbing at his eyes, Louis looked around the crypt. In a corner, he spotted his smashed glasses.

"I . . . can see perfectly," he whispered. He looked at the crypt entranceway. "I guess after all this, I shouldn't be surprised."

Paul stood up, testing his strength. He was bushed but felt fine. "We won, didn't we, Dad?" he asked.

"Sure did, Sparky. Sure did. And when we get back to good old Rochester, you're gonna have to tell me how you did it."

"I had some help," Paul said, smiling at his mother. Then he remembered Abigail and Johnny.

As if reading his thoughts, his mother said, "You'll see them again."

"I don't think so," Paul said. Ever since reawakening into his physical self, Paul had felt somehow different. Lighter, less burdened somehow, as if a lifelong headache had just disappeared. And he was afraid he knew what that meant.

Paul closed his eyes and waited for the curtains to unfold and reveal the darkened screen. Nothing happened. Paul tried to picture the curtains parting, raising, or disappearing. Still nothing. He took a deep, slow breath and tried again, but felt absolutely no connection to the spectral realm. He felt, he realized shockingly, absolutely normal.

"It's . . . gone," he announced softly. The realization was both relieving and disappointing.

His mother hugged him close. "It took a lot of power to win this battle."

"Did we really win?" Paul asked. "Is the devil—really gone?"

Virginia bit a lip, wishing she could believe her own words. "At least for now," she said.

The answer seemed to satisfy Paul. He watched as Martin Hamilton spoke animatedly with the guard.

"Are we in trouble?" Paul asked.

"Tell you what, Sparky," Louis said as he led the way out of the crypt into the light of day. "You let me worry about that, okay?"

"Okay." Paul stopped, turned around, and looked back at the crypt, cementing its features in his memory. It was hard to believe that it was all over: his gift, his curse, his power. All behind him, forever.

He was normal now. Except for one thing, Paul reflected: he knew that life was eternal. And that, when he died, Abigail and Johnny would be there to show him the way to the life beyond life.

That knowledge, and the warmth of his parents' hands in his, was all the comfort a thirteen-year-old boy needed to face the future.

MORE SUSPENSE/THRILLERS FROM BART

☐ 017-8 CODENAME: NEEDLEPOINT by Robert Marsh $3.95
Canada $4.95
☐ 022-4 THE FINAL FOUR by Roy H. Parker $3.95
Canada $4.95
☐ 014-3 THE JOSHUA FACTOR by Donald D. Clayton $3.95
Canada $4.95
☐ 011-9 PROPHET OF TERROR by G. Lee Tippin $3.95
Canada $4.95
☐ 005-4 THE VOICE by Colm Connolly $3.50
Canada $4.50
☐ 047-X THE HONOR O PETER KRAMER by Augusto $3.95
Ferrera Canada $4.95

Buy them at your local bookstore or use this handy coupon:
Clip and mail this page with your order

BART BOOKS
Dept. MO
155 E. 34th Street, 12E
New York, NY 10016

Please send me the book(s) I have checked above. I am enclosing
$_____ (please add $1.00 for the first book and 50¢ for each
additional book to cover postage and handling). Send check or money
order only—no cash or C.O.D.'s.

Mr./Mrs./Ms _____
Address _____
City _____ State/Zip _____
Please allow six weeks for delivery. Prices subject to change without
notice.

MORE SCIENCE FICTION FROM BART

☐ 008-9 BLACK IN TIME by John Jakes $2.95
Canada $3.95

☐ 003-8 MENTION MY NAME IN ATLANTIS by $2.95
John Jakes Canada $3.95

☐ 012-7 THE WORLD JONES MADE by Philip K. Dick $2.95
Canada $3.95

☐ 016-X BART SCIENCE FICTION TRIPLET #1 by $3.50
Isaac Asimov, Gregory Benford, Canada $4.50
Poul Anderson

☐ 032-1 BRING THE JUBILEE by Ward Moore $3.50
Canada $3.95

☐ 037-2 DRAGONS OF LIGHT edited by Orson $3.95
Scott Card Canada $4.95

☐ 033-X DRAGONS OF DARKNESS edited by Orson $3.95
Scott Card Canada $4.95

☐ 046-1 THE DEVIL IS DEAD by R.A. Lafferty $3.50
Canada $4.50

☐ 048-8 FOURTH MANSIONS by R.A. Lafferty $3.50
Canada $4.50

☐ 057-7 MISSING MAN by Katherine MacLean $3.50
Canada $4.50

Buy them at your local bookstore or use this handy coupon:
Clip and mail this page with your order

BART BOOKS
Dept. MO
155 E. 34th Street, 12E
New York, NY 10016

Please send me the book(s) I have checked above. I am enclosing
$_____ (please add $1.00 for the first book and 50¢ for each
additional book to cover postage and handling). Send check or money
order only—no cash or C.O.D.'s.

Mr./Mrs./Ms _____
Address _____
City _____ State/Zip _____
Please allow six weeks for delivery. Prices subject to change without
notice.